"How th [barcode] ne to W about Someone You've Never Even Met!

How dare you expose someone's private life without his knowledge or permission!"

"But I tried to see you many times."

"I'll bet!" he snarled contemptuously as he moved in on her. "And as for your book . . ." He held it up in front of her and opened it to the center. *"This is what I think of it."* With a savage smile, he ripped the book in half as easily as if it had been a single sheet of paper.

A collective gasp went up from the crowd and Arden flinched as if he'd slapped her.

He threw the pieces down on the table and his now charcoal-dark eyes raked her body, making her feel naked and exposed. "I'll be seeing you," he promised ominously.

GINA CAIMI

started making up her own fairy tales when she was six years old. It was the only way she could get through arithmetic class. She sculpts as a hobby, adores the opera, ballet and old movies, but writing remains her major passion. And she still hates arithmetic.

Dear Reader:

SILHOUETTE DESIRE is an exciting new line of contemporary romances from Silhouette Books. During the past year, many Silhouette readers have written in telling us what other types of stories they'd like to read from Silhouette, and we've kept these comments and suggestions in mind in developing SILHOUETTE DESIRE.

DESIREs feature all of the elements you like to see in a romance, plus a more sensual, provocative story. So if you want to experience all the excitement, passion and joy of falling in love, then SILHOUETTE DESIRE is for you.

Karen Solem
Editor-in-Chief
Silhouette Books

GINA CAIMI
Passionate Awakening

Silhouette Desire
Published by Silhouette Books New York
America's Publisher of Contemporary Romance

SILHOUETTE BOOKS, a Division of Simon & Schuster, Inc.
1230 Avenue of the Americas, New York, N.Y. 10020

Distributed by Pocket Books

ISBN: 0-671-49826-6

First Silhouette Books printing March, 1984

10 9 8 7 6 5 4 3 2 1

America's Publisher of Contemporary Romance

Printed in the U.S.A.

BC91

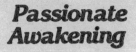

Passionate
Awakening

1

~∞∞∞∞∞∞∞∞∞.

The line of autograph seekers extended far outside the door of the exclusive bookstore, which was never meant to contain so many people. The almost tropical heat and glare of the Miami sunshine pouring through the open door had all but overwhelmed the effects of the air conditioning.

Arden found herself wishing she'd worn her thick, honey-blond hair up in a ponytail instead of letting it spill all over her shoulders and halfway down her back. She tugged self-consciously at her lavender silk dress, which was beginning to stick to her, emphasizing every curve of her lithe but well-rounded body.

Still, she had to admit, in spite of the heat and the Tower of Babel noise surrounding her, she couldn't have been happier over the reception her book was receiving. Even though no one would ever know she'd written it, she was proud of its success.

She ran her long, delicate fingers over a copy of the book as if she still needed to touch it to believe it existed. *Inside Flint Masters: An Intimate Memoir* by Felicia Marlowe. Without realizing it, she wrinkled her nose up at the cover. The title was a scrawl of blood-red lipstick over a glossy photo of suggestively crumpled-up white satin sheets.

Arden had always felt that the art director had gone overboard with the cover. Admittedly, there was a sensational element to the biography which any book about the mysterious Mr. Masters would have to contain, but she had tried to do a serious profile. The artwork only emphasized the lurid elements of Flint Masters's life-style and his previous relationship with Felicia Marlowe. As a lowly ghostwriter, she'd had no say in the matter.

With a resigned sigh, she picked up the stack of books and, easing her way through the crowd of mostly women, set them down at the other end of the long, rectangular table where Felicia was autographing one book after another with a flourish.

Arden had never seen Felicia looking lovelier or more excited. Her bottle green eyes glittered as if she were running a fever, and her unusually white skin was so flushed that it almost matched her flaming red hair. She'd obviously forgotten a model's cardinal rule and was using every muscle in her face as she smiled and chatted with uncharacteristic animation. Her normally aloof facade was rapidly crumbling under the delicious onslaught of adulation.

Arden really couldn't blame her. She wondered whether she'd be immune to all that attention, then decided that the question was academic.

She bent over the table and was busy verifying the latest sales figures when a huge hand suddenly thrust a copy of the book under her nose and a deep, gravelly voice asked—no, demanded—that she autograph it for him.

Caught in the middle of adding a long column of figures—one of her lesser talents—Arden waved her pen impatiently in Felicia's direction.

"You're Arden Stuart, aren't you?" the voice insisted.

"Yes," she sighed irritably, annoyed because he'd made her forget the number she had just carried; now she'd have to add the figures all over again. She looked up reluctantly, and the question she started to ask him not only died on her lips, but flew clear out of her head.

Maybe if she'd seen him from a distance she might have been prepared for the heart-stopping sight of him. But to be suddenly confronted by well over six feet of sheer virility towering over her left her stunned and incapable of hiding her immediate gut response to him.

He was wearing a raw silk safari suit which had to have been custom-made because it fit every curve of his muscular body to perfection. Like the cloth, Arden's sapphire blue eyes followed the lines of his wide shoulders and chest as they tapered down to a narrow waist, surprisingly lean hips, and a clear outline of taut, muscular legs.

A self-satisfied smile creased his ruggedly handsome face, and the proud, almost arrogant look he gave her told her that he'd read every thought and emotion he had just set churning inside her.

Arden blushed from the ground up but she couldn't take her eyes off him, let alone talk or move. He seemed to be in his late thirties, but had the look of a man who's lived several lifetimes. His deep-set eyes were a startling shade of silvery gray, made even more striking by his deep copper tan. The thick, blue-black hair which tumbled onto his forehead had a white streak slashing through it just to one side.

His strange, piercing eyes broke contact with hers, then deliberately, brazenly scanned her body, lingering on her high, rounded breasts and the outline her thighs made against the damp skirt that was clinging to them. His smile turned provocative, making her aware of the invitation which could be read into the curve her buttocks made as she leaned over the table.

Arden straightened up like a shot, feeling confused, shamed, excited, and insulted all at the same time. And furious as hell with him for making her feel this way, especially since he was obviously enjoying it so much.

Struggling to get herself back under control, she turned and walked around the end of the table. Somehow she felt safer with the full width of the table between them and was able to look up at him again.

"Yes? I'm Arden Stuart," she said in her most professional tone of voice, determined to ignore the intense way he was looking at her, even though it went right through her. She forced a polite smile. "Is there something I can do for you?"

His eyes darkened to a steel gray and something inside him seemed to pull back, shut down, as if he'd suddenly remembered why he was there. "I'd like your autograph." He tossed the book he was still clutching in his huge hand onto the table in front of her.

"*My* autograph?" She laughed. "I'm afraid you made a mistake."

He started, then glared at her like a man who was not used to making mistakes—or having anyone tell him if he did.

"I mean, you've got the wrong party." She pointed to the far end of the table where Felicia was sitting, partly hidden by the people still crowding around her. "You want Miss Marlowe . . . over there."

"I know who I want," he said carefully, in that deep, raspy voice of his. Arden wondered just what he meant by that, till he added, "*You're* the one who wrote the book, aren't you?"

"What?" she stammered. How on earth could he know that? There were only two people in the whole world besides her who knew: Felicia and her editor.

"You're not ashamed to admit it, are you?" he taunted.

"No, of course not," she said defensively and, with a proud toss of her honey-blond hair, reached for the book.

"Who shall I dedicate it to?" she asked coldly.

"To Flint Masters."

His words cracked like a gunshot, reverberating throughout the bookstore. Arden's eyes widened as the blood rushed to her face, pounding at her temples. The only sound in the entire store now was a series of uncontrollable gasps, like hiccups, coming from Felicia.

Turning his head slowly, Flint Masters looked over at her with such withering contempt that the last gasp shriveled up in her throat and Felicia turned chalk white. Dismissing her as someone too low to deal with, he turned his withering gaze back to Arden.

She stood there, the pen still frozen in her hand, aware that everyone in the store was watching them, breathlessly waiting to see what would happen next.

"Flint Masters," he repeated caustically. "F—l—i—n . . ."

"I know how to spell it," Arden snapped back, even though she was shaking inside. She refused to let him browbeat her as he had Felicia.

A surprised smile curved his mouth and she thought she caught a glimmer of reluctant respect in his eyes before she bent over the book. Without a second's hesitation, she scribbled the first thought that came to mind. She handed the volume back to him, looking straight into those incredible eyes even though the coldness and barely suppressed anger she saw there unnerved her.

He scanned the inscription before reading it aloud. "'To Flint Masters. It was nice *not* knowing you. Arden Stuart.' So you admit, Miss Stuart," he prompted, as if he were the prosecuting attorney and she were on trial for her life, "that you've never met me before today?" He held the book up so everyone could see the inscription—Exhibit A.

"No . . . I mean . . . yes, I admit . . ."

"Then how the hell do you presume to write a book about someone you've never even met! How dare you expose someone's private life without his knowledge or permission!"

"But I . . . I tried to see you . . . many times, but . . ."

"I bet!" he snarled contemptuously as he moved in on her. He was so close that she could smell his tangy, masculine scent, and feel his warm breath on her skin. "Well, now you've seen me. And it won't be the last you see of me, I promise you.

"As for your book . . ." Holding it up in front of her with those huge, powerful hands, he opened it to the center. "I've already read it. And *this* is what I think of it." With a savage smile, he ripped the book in half as easily as if it were a single sheet of paper. A collective gasp went up from the crowd and Arden flinched as if he'd slapped her.

He threw the pieces down on the table and his now charcoal-dark eyes raked her body, making her feel naked and exposed. "I'll be seeing you," he promised ominously.

Turning away abruptly, he started for the door, the stunned crowd parting before him like the Red Sea.

2

~@@@@@@@@@@@.

Arden was so deeply shaken by her meeting with Flint Masters that she couldn't go on working. Felicia was very understanding and insisted that Arden take the rest of the afternoon off. She even offered her the use of her car so Arden could do a little sightseeing, something she'd been too busy to do since they got to Miami.

At first, she was surprised by this display of friendship on Felicia's part—the first since they started the book tour over two months ago. Later, she realized, the ex-cover girl had obviously felt responsible for what happened.

Arden thanked her but declined the offer. She felt sure that the state she was in would prevent her from even seeing, let alone enjoying, the sights. She might even end up wrapping the brand-new Coupe de Ville around a pole with herself in it.

Her head was throbbing, her whole body ached, and no matter how hard she tried, she couldn't shake a feeling of the most total humiliation. All she wanted was to get as far away from the store and the gawking customers as she could get.

The first thing she did when she got back to the hotel was close all the drapes, shutting out the painful glare of the sun and muffling the insistent sounds of the street traffic which carried all the way up to the sixth floor and grated on her raw nerves.

Her face was still flushed; her body burned as if she had a fever. Rushing over to the air-conditioner, she turned it up to high and, lifting her thick, damp hair on top of her head, placed herself directly in front of it.

She closed her eyes, giving herself up to the refreshing feeling of the artificial breeze which was plastering her damp dress against her skin. The memory of Masters's silver gray glance moving hungrily over her body flashed in her mind. She shivered.

With an exasperated sigh, Arden let her hair tumble back down over her shoulders, hugged herself to keep from shaking, and moved out of direct range of the air-conditioner . . . as if she were actually shivering from the cold!

A feeling of angry confusion swept over her. She didn't recognize herself. She wasn't an immature sixteen-year-old, after all, but a usually self-possessed young woman of twenty-six who was used to admiring glances from men. She'd never seen a man look at her like that, however, and never had a look had such an effect on her. She'd never seen a man quite like him, either. If only she had known what to expect!

Since he consistently refused to have his picture taken, she hadn't been able to find one. Apparently, neither had anyone else, she soon discovered during her research. Not even the wire services had been able to track a photo down for her.

She had tried to get Felicia to give her a detailed description of him, but apart from stating the obvious, that he was "extremely attractive for a millionaire," she'd been rather vague. So Arden had found herself creating her own image of the elusive Mr. Masters out of all the bits and pieces she was able to collect from Felicia and the others she'd interviewed.

She told herself, at the time, that she had to create this fantasy image of him in order to be able to write about him. Now she wasn't so sure that was the real reason. And she found herself questioning Felicia's motives as well.

Had she really loved him for what he was? Or had she been merely dazzled by his money and power? How else could she have been so vague about him? Arden had seen him only once—and never intended to see him again—but she knew that every feature of his face, the gravel and velvet sound of his voice, even the forceful way he moved would be imprinted on her brain forever. Nothing Felicia had told her, not even her own wildest fantasies, had prepared her for the intense sexuality he projected . . . and evoked. Arden had never experienced anything like it. Not even with Neil. Up to an hour ago, she didn't even know such feelings existed.

"Why?" she murmured. "Why, out of all the men in this world, did *he* have to turn out to be Flint Masters?"

She shook her head angrily, as if to shake off all thoughts of him. A nice, cool shower was what she needed right about now, she decided impulsively. She quickly peeled off her dress and lacy under-things and, stopping only to retrieve her robe from the foot of the bed, rushed into the bathroom.

She turned the water on full blast, hoping the sound would drown out the gravelly voice darkly promising "I'll be seeing you" over and over in her mind. And this time the shiver that went through her was one of fear. She recalled the savage smile that had twisted his mouth as he ripped the book apart. Arden truly believed that *she* was the one he'd wanted to rip apart with those huge hands.

Slipping out of the robe, she stepped into the shower and the cool, welcome freshness of the water. She let it pour over her upturned face and hair and spill down her body, washing the sticky perspiration right off her. But she still felt tense and achy.

She adjusted the water so that steaming hot needles massaged the tension out of her. If only she could get rid of the underlying anxiety so easily.

If she could only figure out what he'd meant about seeing her again. Did he mean he'd be seeing her in court? Or was he planning another dreadful scene in public? And why did he want to see *her* anyway? Felicia was the one he should be furious with. *She* was the one who'd been so eager to tell all. The book had not even been Arden's idea.

As a matter of fact, when Susan Jackson, a senior editor at one of the newer, more aggressive publishing houses, had approached her, she was very surprised. She had done a series of personality profiles for several magazines, and they had been very well received, but she'd never written a book before. She'd always wanted to, of course, so when Susan offered her the chance to write one about Flint Masters, "the elusive tycoon," she jumped at it. Who wouldn't have?

He'd been dubbed "the elusive tycoon" by the frustrated media. His meteoric rise from out of nowhere and his stunning successes had been well documented, but nothing was known about his personal life since no one had ever succeeded in getting so much as an interview out of him. It was a challenge Arden found impossible to resist.

Ever since she was a child, Arden had been fascinated by other people and their behavior. She often joked that if she hadn't become a writer, she might have been a psychiatrist. She had an insatiable curiosity about what made people tick and a natural gift for getting them to open up and reveal deeply personal truths about themselves. Solving a puzzle as intricate as Flint Masters definitely appealed to her.

But there was another, more personal, reason why she'd accepted the assignment. She'd just been through one of the most traumatic experiences of her life and desperately needed something she could get completely involved in—something positive to restore her shattered self-confidence and help her forget what happened with Neil just weeks before so . . .

Arden turned the water off abruptly, her train of thought derailed by a sudden realization: she sounded as though she were building her defense, trying to justify what she had done.

She grabbed a bath towel off the rack and started drying herself forcefully. She hadn't done anything to apologize for, and she refused to let him make her feel guilty. Flint Masters had made himself a public figure through his achievements and through the sheer force of his own personality. He should have known it's always open season on celebrities. She was only doing her job.

Satisfied by the logic of her argument, Arden started towel-drying her hair, telling herself that she was not going to worry about Flint Masters.

Writing about him had been enough. Looking back on it now, she wondered whether Sue Jackson had been right, after all: had she become obsessed with the man?

Arden shook her head so forcefully that her wild, wet, tangled mass of hair whipped around her face and neck. As she methodically set to making it manageable again with the help of her brush and blow-dryer, she repeated to herself what she'd always told Susan. It was impossible to live inside someone else's skin, day in and day out, for almost two years without becoming totally involved. It happens to most writers.

There were, however, times when she felt more like a detective or an archeologist than a writer. The most frustrating part of her search for Flint Masters was that the bits and pieces she finally managed to dig up about him never did form a coherent picture. There were just too many contradictions.

Which man was he? The ruthless tycoon who bought up failing businesses the way other men bought ties? Or the concerned citizen who gave away unpublicized millions to charity and whose benefit and pension plans for his workers were nothing less than revolutionary?

Was the man who'd worked side by side with his own laborers the same one who'd bought a private island where he could isolate himself from the rest of the world? And how do you begin to reconcile the man who instituted free day-care centers for working mothers in all his offices with the playboy who changed high-fashion models as casually as he changed car models?

Arden sighed in frustration and pulled the plug on the blow-dryer. She had thought that once the book was finished she would be through trying to figure out the perversely complicated Mr. Masters!

She glared at herself in the steamed-up mirror, but the image she saw in the haze looked back at her with sardonic silver gray eyes and a mocking smile. Grabbing a towel, she wiped the mirror clean, but she couldn't wipe away the blush she now saw burning her face.

She told herself she was just flushed from the hot shower and the steam which still hung in the air and glistened all over her skin. The bathroom suddenly felt too close and confining. She pulled open the door, welcoming the unexpected rush of chilled air.

She'd planned on taking a nap after her shower but now even the bedroom seemed too confining; yet, she felt strangely lost in it. It was decorated in the most aggressively cheerful shades of yellow and orange. The flowery chintz drapes and matching bedspread tried desperately to give the room a "homey" look but gave off that stale, hotel disinfectant smell instead. And there was something vaguely sad about the rickety rattan tables with their seashell-covered lamps and the flat, lifeless prints on the walls.

Arden switched on the TV set, more to fill the void of silence than anything else. The calming effect of the shower was quickly dissipating, leaving her tense again. She tried concentrating on the six o'clock news but was unable to block out the disturbing thoughts still crowding her mind.

The last thing she needed, Arden decided as she headed for the closet, was to spend another evening watching television, or another minute thinking about the impossible Mr. Masters. What she needed was to get out for a change, to be around people. She just couldn't understand why this man—whom she didn't really know, and liked even less—should have such an effect on her.

While she dressed, Arden reasoned that the only logical explanation was that she'd never solved the puzzle of Flint Masters to her own satisfaction. Maybe if she'd succeeded in capturing him the way she'd wanted . . .

"And whose fault was that?" she muttered under her breath as she struggled with the hoop earrings she'd bought to go with the colorful gypsy outfit she was wearing. She'd tried to get in touch with him any number of times so he could tell his side of the story and because—she wasn't ashamed to admit it—she longed to see for herself what kind of man he really was. But he didn't even have the courtesy to return her phone calls. So now, if he felt her portrait of him was one-sided and not all that flattering, he had no one to blame but himself!

Feeling thoroughly vindicated, Arden paused to look at herself in the dresser mirror. Because of the steam in the bathroom, her hair was a mass of golden curls. Her cheeks were still quite flushed so she didn't need any blusher. A touch of mascara and some lip gloss were all that was needed. As she applied them a nagging thought in the back of her mind kept tugging at her.

The reason he was furious with her wasn't that she'd painted an unflattering portrait of him. From what little she'd seen of him, Arden felt sure he was a man who cared nothing about what other people thought of him.

No, she realized as she reached for the lip gloss, he was furious with her because she had invaded the privacy which he valued above everything else. She'd always wondered whether there was a very real but secret reason why he was so determined to hide his past.

Whatever it was, Arden knew instinctively, he would never forgive her for what she'd done. And he'd find some way to make her pay for it. She remembered his promise to see her again.

Arden fixed the smear she had just made with her lipstick brush and carefully redrew the line.

Flint Masters might still be an enigma to her, but there was one thing about him she felt sure of: he was a man who kept his promises.

3

As Arden waited for the elevator, she felt a small sense of relief that they would only be in Miami two more days. The book tour would be over then and she'd be going back home to New York and the vacation she needed even more than she'd realized.

She moved through the open doors and pushed the button marked Lobby, making a mental note to call Felicia first thing tomorrow morning. They would have to get someone else to work as backup during the autographings because she wasn't about to risk another encounter with Flint Masters.

As she stepped out into the lobby, Arden caught

herself automatically scanning the crowd of people milling about. She sighed impatiently at this sign of incipient paranoia, a disease she'd never shown any signs of until now, and reminded herself that, although ads about the bookstore autographings had run in all the newspapers, there was no way he could know where she was staying. As long as she avoided the bookstore, there was no way he could find her, she reassured herself.

Pulling her lace shawl around her, she walked resolutely through the lobby to the revolving doors. Once outside, she hesitated again. She'd meant to go to that little seafood restaurant where she'd been dining almost every night. It was small and cozy, and she didn't feel so conspicuous sitting at a table all by herself. Now she wondered whether she should try someplace new. Felicia had recommended a terrific Cuban restaurant that one of her new admirers had taken her to, and it was just down the street.

Realizing that she was blocking the entrance, Arden moved to one side to clear the way for a porter lugging several valises. A lovely young couple followed close behind. From the shyly ecstatic look on their faces and the intense way they were holding hands, Arden guessed they were honeymooners. She watched them wistfully for a moment before continuing over to the end of the striped canopy where she peered up and down Biscayne Boulevard.

She was trying to remember whether the Cuban restaurant was to the right or to the left when the door of a pearl gray Silver Spirit parked by the curb suddenly swung open. She stepped to one side to let the occupants out but a powerful hand reached out and grabbed her wrist. She started to cry out but the sound froze in her throat when she saw the hard-as-granite eyes of Flint Masters glaring up at her.

"I've been waiting for you," he muttered impatiently, as if they had a date and she'd taken too long to dress. "Get in." It was an order, not an invitation. "Get in!"

"I will not," Arden gasped as she struggled to free her wrist.

He tightened his hold and his fingers dug into her flesh. "I just want to talk to you," he insisted.

"Well, I don't want to talk to you!" She was still fighting to free herself but his grip was too strong for her. "Will you let go of me?" she cried angrily while she looked around, hoping to find someone who would help her.

Several people walking by looked over at them, but from the smiles on their faces she realized that they assumed the two of them were having a lovers' quarrel, which only compounded the absurdity of the situation and her frustration.

"Stop acting like a little idiot and get in the car," he muttered dangerously as he tugged on her arm.

Arden wasn't sure which she was more afraid of: getting in the car with him or risking another embarrassing scene in public.

"We can talk another time," she tried appeasing him. "I . . . I've got someplace to go now and . . ."

"You don't have anyplace else to go," he snapped impatiently, "except to a restaurant all by yourself."

She was so amazed that he would know this about her that she stopped struggling for a moment. That was all he needed. He pulled her down and into the car all in one easy motion. Caught off-balance, Arden ended up sprawled all over him, her legs tangled up in his, her breasts pressed hard against his powerful chest. Her startled mouth was so close to his that she swallowed the ragged breath he'd exhaled sharply on contact and gasped as she tasted the warm sweetness of it.

Her head snapped back but the disturbingly male scent of his skin followed. She wanted to yell at him to let go of her but the pulse at the base of her throat was beating so violently she couldn't even swallow. Wedging her shaking hands between them, she pushed against his chest with all her strength and felt his muscles tauten under the blue silk shirt, sending unaccustomed ripples of feeling all through her.

"Why are you fighting me?" He laughed sardonically, his warm breath brushing her lips again as his arms locked around her, pulling her back to him. "I'm only trying to help you." He lifted her easily, taking the full weight of her body on his before shifting her off him and dumping her unceremoniously onto the seat next to him.

"Just what . . . do you think . . . you're doing?" Arden stuttered angrily as she attempted to pull herself up from the plush depths of the suede-upholstered seat with as much dignity as she could manage under the circumstances.

"Why? What did you think I was doing?" He grinned suggestively. His smoke gray glance skimmed her exposed legs from ankle to thigh, making her feel painfully self-conscious as she struggled to pull her tangled skirt back into place. Her mind was a jumble of mixed emotions. The fact that he not only was aware of the effect he had on her but was thoroughly enjoying it added to her angry confusion.

His self-satisfied grin turned abruptly into a frown and he glared at her as if she'd deliberately distracted him from his original purpose. "I told you . . ." He turned away from her to push one of the multicolored buttons on the panel next to him. "I want to talk to you."

"And I told you, I have nothing to say to you," Arden snapped as the car door slammed shut behind her with a solid click. Wheeling around, she grabbed onto the handle but no matter which way she turned it, she couldn't get the door open. Her eyes widened in amazement as she looked over at him. The smug look on his ruggedly handsome face confirmed her suspicion: the door was locked from his side.

"Open this door," she insisted in a voice she hoped carried far more assurance than she was feeling.

Without changing expression, he pressed another button and nonchalantly ordered, "Once around the park, Albert."

The chauffeur nodded in agreement from the other side of the glass partition before he shifted into drive and began steering the car away from the curb.

"No . . . stop the car!" Arden called out to him, but he continued maneuvering the Rolls smoothly into traffic without acknowledging her. "Please . . . stop this car!"

"He can't hear you without the intercom," Flint Masters stated matter-of-factly, scrunching down into his seat as if he were settling in for a long ride. "And even if he did, I give the orders around here."

"Then you'd better order him to stop this car . . . right now," Arden demanded, hoping he wouldn't hear the edge of panic in her voice.

"Afraid?" he taunted.

"No . . . of course not," she lied.

"You should be afraid." He smiled harshly. "If you were a man, for what you did, I'd have broken every bone in your body."

Remembering the savage way he'd ripped the book apart with his bare hands, she didn't doubt him for a moment.

"But since it's pretty obvious you're not a man," he added dryly, smoky eyes raking her body, "you don't have to be afraid of that."

"I'm not afraid of anything," Arden said defiantly. "I just don't like being taken for a ride."

"Nobody does," he shot back.

Turning away from his accusing look, she glanced out the window just as the Rolls completed a sharp turn off the main avenue onto a dimly lit one-way street. A knot of apprehension tightened in her stomach even though she told herself that a man in his position could scarely afford to do something foolish.

"Don't worry, we're not going to throw you off the deep end of a pier," he said as though he'd read her mind. "Albert's just getting away from all this traffic."

Furious at his know-it-all attitude, Arden turned on him. "What is this all about, anyway? What do you want from me?"

He seemed either amused by her anger, or else too sure of himself to take her seriously. "What do you think I want?"

"How should I know? You're the one who . . . kidnapped me. You tell me!"

"I'm not kidnapping you," he protested. "This is the only way I could get to talk to you. I wanted to call you up to ask for a . . . an appointment, but I knew you'd hang up on me after what happened this afternoon. I am right, aren't I?"

She had to admit that he was, but she was damned if she was going to give him the satisfaction. "You didn't answer my question."

"What question?"

"What do you want from me?"

"What . . . do . . . I . . . want . . . from . . . you," he repeated slowly to himself, savoring the endless possibilities. He stretched his long legs out in front of him, hard muscles straining against his jeans, and stared thoughtfully at his snakeskin boots. A smile played on his lips before he looked up at her again. "What are you offering?" he teased, but the look in his smoke gray eyes was so piercingly sensual it went right through her.

Her body stiffened against the strange quivering inside her. "Do you always do that? Answer a question with another question?"

"Do I really do that?" He laughed mockingly, but she wasn't sure whether he was making fun of her or himself. She wasn't sure of anything where he was concerned, Arden realized. He shifted gears as smoothly as the car and she was having trouble keeping up with him.

"I didn't realize I did that." He shrugged it off.

"That's funny. I got the impression you did it deliberately."

A frown of annoyance hardened his face again, warning her not to pursue this any further.

"It's certainly an effective way of not having to answer . . . to anyone but yourself."

He studied her intently for a moment, the way a scientist might study a totally foreign object under his microscope.

"You're very perceptive, aren't you?" he said finally, but the way he said it, it sounded like an insult.

To Arden, it was the highest compliment he could have paid her because it proved that she'd finally succeeded in getting to him. She couldn't resist rubbing it in.

"You don't like perceptive women, do you?" she asked.

"Would you like a drink?" he answered. He pushed another button on the console and a panel under the glass partition slid open, revealing an eighteen-inch TV screen, a stereo, and a well-stocked bar, complete with portable ice machine.

"Nothing for me . . . thank you."

"Not even a Pernod?" he inquired casually and waited for the shock to register on her face. "I thought that was your favorite drink."

Arden gasped. "How do you know that?"

"You'd be surprised how much I know about you." He shrugged matter-of-factly, but he couldn't conceal the victorious gleam in his eyes. "You're twenty-six years old," he went on to prove his point as he fixed them both drinks, "originally from Utica. After losing both your parents and a younger brother in a car accident when you were twelve, you were raised by a series of relatives." He paused as he replaced the bottle of Pernod and reached for the club soda. "This is only a guess, but I'm willing to bet it was about that time you started writing." He peered over his shoulder at her. "Am I right?"

Arden nodded dumbly and he turned his attention back to mixing the drinks.

"After working your way through college," he continued in the same flat, clinical tone of voice, "you moved to New York where you share an apartment on the Upper East Side with two other girls." He twisted a lime peel into one of the drinks before offering it to her with a truly perverse smile. "312 East Ninety-sixth Street, apartment 4G."

Arden was too stunned to react, let alone move, and he had to practically shove the glass into her hand. The movement freed her somehow. She pulled herself up, even managed to force a smile because she refused to admit to him—or was it to herself?—just how vulnerable his knowing so much about her made her feel.

"Well, you've certainly done your homework, as my editor used to say . . . lime and all," she joked feebly.

"I'm just getting to the best part." He raised his glass in a toast. "Here's to Neil Foster."

Arden flinched as if he'd hit her, and spilled some of the drink in her lap. The blood drained from her face, leaving it as icy cold as the liquid gluing her skirt to her thighs. She couldn't say or do anything except stare back at him in shocked pain.

"I see the suave Mr. Foster still has an effect on you," he muttered sarcastically as if that bothered him somehow. "Getting back to 'This is your life, Arden Stuart,'" he continued relentlessly while tugging a handkerchief out of his back pocket, "four years ago, you became engaged to said Neil Foster. A charmer if ever there was one, I'm told." He started dabbing at the spill on her dress. Arden wanted to protest but couldn't. "Two days before the wedding, he called the whole thing off. Threw you over for the boss's daughter who had . . ."

"Stop it!" She pushed his hand away so violently that the handkerchief flew clear across the car.

A victorious smile lit up his ruggedly handsome face again, and now she was sorry she'd given him the satisfaction of seeing how deeply he'd hurt her. But the crazy thing was, *his* knowing about Neil was what hurt the most. She turned her face away, so he wouldn't see the tears of humiliation filling her eyes, and stared blindly out the window.

"How does it feel?" his mocking voice pursued her. "What's it like having a complete stranger digging into your private life, exposing your most intimate memories?"

Arden buried herself in the drink. She felt so ashamed, so totally stripped emotionally, that she didn't know how she could ever face him again. But now she understood the bitter rage that made him want to lash out because she felt exactly the same way.

"So how does it feel?" he taunted her again.

She turned on him furiously. "Every bit as painful and humiliating as you wanted it to feel!"

"Now you know how the other half lives."

"Don't put me in the same class with you," she snapped contemptuously.

He went white under his tan; his silvery eyes narrowed dangerously as his hand clenched automatically into a fist. For a moment Arden thought he might actually hit her but even that couldn't have stopped her.

"*I* never tried to deliberately hurt . . . anyone! I tried to be fair and gave you every chance to tell your side of the story. You were the one who never returned my calls!"

"What . . . calls?"

"What calls? If I called you once, I called you ten times!"

"Sure." His blunt tone ruthlessly dismissed her as a liar.

"But I did. Honestly. I wanted to meet you. . . ." Arden caught herself, but too late.

"Really?" The amused smile that curved his sensuous mouth told her he'd picked up on the intense feeling which had slipped out to her own amazement.

"Because of the book," she insisted, while turning five different shades of red because she knew he didn't believe that one either. "Anyway, you were never available when I called," she rattled on compulsively, "but I always left a message."

"I never got any messages."

"Well, don't blame me if you've got a lousy

secretary!" she exploded. She'd never felt so totally frustrated. She took several gulps of her drink, hoping it would help her to calm down. She had never met anyone who could get under her skin as he did with just a word or a look.

The look he was now giving her over his drink was part surprise, part doubt. She could feel him carefully weighing this unexpected piece of evidence and wondered whether or not he would decide in her favor. It bothered her that she cared.

Determined not to show it, Arden buried herself in her drink again. "I don't know why you're taking this out on me. The book was Felicia's idea, you know . . . not mine."

"Felicia?" He laughed contemptuously. "Felicia could never have written that book. The only things she knows how to write are checks." Reaching over abruptly, he grabbed the glass she was nervously fiddling with right out of her hands and forced her to look him full in the face.

"No, it was you all right," he said, smiling ominously. Without taking his eyes off her, he thrust both glasses back onto their magnetized coasters.

Arden hadn't realized that she'd been holding onto hers like the proverbial drowning man clutching a straw and now she felt strangely naked, defenseless, without it.

"Sure, Felicia was the one who supplied you with all the gossip," he accused, moving in on her physically as well, "the kind of half-truths and distorted facts her not very bright but greedy little mind knew would sell. But you . . ." He moved closer still. His face was barely inches away, his muscular thigh hard up against the full length of hers. "You were the one who filled in all the rest . . . all that pseudopsychological Freudian crap!"

The impact of his towering presence in such a confined space was overwhelming. There was no way she could fight it. She felt under attack—not only from the bitter anger of his words but also from the soft, warm explosions of breath they made on her skin. The rich, tangy scent of him was assaulting her senses, and the barely suppressed emotion that stiffened every muscle of his powerful body sent a current of raw electricity shooting right through hers.

"What gives you the right to get into someone else's head?" he demanded. "To dig into someone else's innermost thoughts and feelings and . . ."

He stopped cold, as if he'd said more than he'd intended.

To Arden, this was the final shocker. So that was it: she'd obviously guessed some deeply personal truth about him. She searched his face in the flickering light of the streetlamps which filtered through the windows and was stunned by what she saw written there. She never would have believed him capable of such naked vulnerability.

She reached out impulsively to touch his arm but her hand froze in midair like the words of explanation she'd started to utter. A remorseless pride had hardened his face again, denying the look she'd caught, warning her that he intended paying her back for what she'd done to him. She suddenly felt very tired.

"I don't know what you want from me." She sighed wearily as she sank back against the sofalike seat. "The book has already been published. There's nothing I can do about that. What kind of satisfaction can I possibly give you at this point?"

The suggestive smile that played on his lips as his silver gray eyes slowly, deliberately traced every curve of her body forced her to acknowledge the double meaning in her question while answering it at the same time. Furious at him for distorting the meaning of her words and shifting gears again, throwing her off-balance, Arden pulled herself up proudly. "The only satisfaction you'll ever get from me, Flint Masters, will be in court. So go ahead, call in your battery of lawyers and . . ."

"What battery of lawyers?"

"The battery of lawyers I'm sure you always use to get what you want from people who don't have the money or power that you do!"

"What are you talking about?" He smiled patronizingly at the absurdity of her statement, which made her even angrier.

"Go ahead then, sue me," she taunted, "if you're so determined to get even with me!"

"I know a better way." He laughed and, grabbing her impulsively, pulled her against him as his mouth pressed down on hers. Arden pulled back against the suede seat with a muffled cry of surprise but his body followed, crushing hers softly, blocking out any chance of escape.

Before she could recover, his kiss deepened, and what had been a mere impulse became overwhelmingly intense, as if it had been coiled up inside him all along, tightening like a spring and, at the touch of her, had finally snapped out of his control.

Unable to free herself, Arden started thrashing her head from side to side in a desperate attempt to break away from him and from the strange, unsettling feelings he was arousing in her. His mouth finally lifted from hers but only because he was out of breath. His hands still held her tight and his astonished eyes promised more.

"Let go . . . of me," she managed to gasp, her voice shaking almost as much as she was. "How . . . dare you . . . do this?"

"Consider it settling out of court." He laughed breathlessly. "I never did like lawyers." He ran his hands playfully up and down her arms, trailing shivery goose bumps behind him.

"Stop . . . this car! Right now! I want to get out!" She pulled her shaking hands away, angrily.

"Why? I thought you wanted that as much as I did," he teased.

"What? That's ridiculous. . . ." For once in her life Arden was at a total loss for words. Probably because part of her, the part that could still feel the imprint of his body burning on hers, knew he was right. She couldn't recognize herself in the way she was acting and that upset her. All she felt sure of was that she had to get out of that car and as far away from him as possible.

Sitting up abruptly, she started to call out to the chauffeur to stop the car when she remembered that he couldn't hear her. She started waving frantically at him through the partition in a determined effort to get his attention even though she felt like a complete and utter idiot.

"He can't see you, you know," Flint Masters's

amused voice informed her from behind. "That's one-way glass."

Arden's flailing arms froze in midair. Part of her was greatly relieved that the chauffeur hadn't seen what just happened, but the other part felt worse than ever because that meant that she was, for all intents and purposes, completely alone with him in the dark, confining intimacy of the car. Her hands fell awkwardly into her lap as if she were a puppet and someone had just cut the strings.

"How convenient," she managed to toss curtly over her shoulder, "and isn't it just like you to have a car like this."

A flash of anger streaked across his face before he deliberately turned away from her and pushed the intercom button on the panel. "Albert, Ms. Stuart is ready to go back to the hotel now," he ordered emotionlessly. The face he turned back to her was equally expressionless except for a tiny vein which beat violently in his jaw.

"This isn't my car," he said evenly. "I didn't take mine with me on this trip."

"What?"

"Sorry to wreck your image of me," he added sarcastically as the Rolls went smoothly into a U-turn. "It happens to be the company car. The reason for all this . . ." The wave of his hand took in the console and partition. "There are such things in the big, bad business world as industrial spies, you know."

His explanation couldn't have been more reasonable or his sincerity more obvious, and Arden realized that she'd been overreacting to him again. She was forced to admit that if she hadn't been so upset, or had had time to think, she would have known a man like him didn't need phony tricks to seduce a woman. She was sure there were plenty of women only too eager to succumb to his obvious charm and the sensual intensity he projected so potently.

He must have caught the contrite look on her face because he suddenly broke into a low and very sexy laugh. "Who knows? There may have been times when it *was* used for . . . the purpose you had in mind."

The smile that lingered on his beautiful mouth was so brazenly suggestive and made him look so impossibly, infuriatingly attractive that she wanted to hit him.

"The purpose . . . *I* had in mind? *You're* the one who practically . . . attacked me . . . not the other way around!"

"You still insist you didn't want me to kiss you?" He frowned as if he were disappointed in her somehow. "Why can't you admit you wanted it as much as I did?"

"I realize you're used to women throwing themselves at you," she said, trying to sound as arrogantly sure of herself as he was, "so this may come as a blow to your colossal ego, but I don't find you attractive at all . . . just the opposite."

"Really?" He flashed his most devastating smile at her and she felt her knees go weak even though she was sitting down. "You have no . . . feeling for me at all then?"

"No. None."

"None?" he mocked. "I leave you totally cold?"

"Totally."

"I see. So if I were to do . . . this . . ." He reached over and softly brushed her lips with his. "It has no effect on you at all?"

Her body stiffened automatically, but she managed a determined, "No."

"And this?" He nipped her bottom lip with his teeth, drawing it into his mouth where his tongue flicked over it lightly.

Arden pulled back as if she'd been burned, then caught herself and shrugged. "No way. Sorry." She shook her head defiantly at his disbelieving grin, sending her long, golden curls flying. Reaching out, he caught clusters of them in both hands and used them to draw her startled face back to his.

"What about this?" he growled softly.

"Look, this is really getting silly . . ." she started to say but he swallowed up the rest of the sentence with his mouth while his huge hands swallowed up her face.

Her heart jumped clear into her throat and she thought she would melt, but she willed herself to go as limp as a rag doll. Fighting him had only made things worse before, so she felt sure that once he realized he wasn't going to get any reaction from her, he would have to let her go. She just hoped he couldn't feel the way she was shaking inside.

There was none of that hungry urgency in his kiss this time. His lips were all softness and warmth, and instead of overwhelming her, his tongue was now teasing her playfully, expertly, sending waves of pleasure all through her—waves she could drown in so easily if she let herself.

Arden fought to hold back even as she ached to kiss him as she'd never kissed or even longed to kiss anyone in her whole life. She couldn't believe this was happening to her, that anyone could have such an effect on her. She didn't know how much more of this she could take but she stifled the urge to push him away because that would be admitting to the almost frightening feelings he was churning up inside her.

Her plan wasn't working at all as she'd intended. Instead of turning him off, her deliberate coldness only goaded him on. He seemed determined to make her respond to him . . . or maybe he sensed the latent hunger he'd awakened inside her, because he escalated his artful attack on her senses.

Strong, demanding arms closed around her, pulling her hard up against him. His tongue wasn't teasing anymore, was suddenly playing for real as it searched out the moist depths of her mouth, opening her up to sensations she'd never experienced before, had never even dreamed existed. She could feel her self-control starting to slip away and only her fear of him held her back. But suddenly *he* seemed unable to hold back anymore. His kiss turned intense and, losing its technical efficiency, started going out of control.

He pulled away, releasing Arden so abruptly that she fell back against the seat. Shaking visibly, she was unable to pretend otherwise in order to defend herself against the victorious smirk she expected to see on his face. To her amazement, he seemed even more dazed than she was.

"My God, but you're delicious," he muttered between clenched teeth, as if he hadn't counted on that, and when he pulled her back to him it seemed to be in spite of himself, but he kissed her like he wanted to drink her all up.

Her mouth opened under his all by itself, inviting him inside.

"That's it . . . that's what I want," he growled as powerful arms pulled her on top of him and wrapped themselves around her. Surrounded, she could feel herself sinking mindlessly into the overwhelming warmth of his mouth and body.

"No," she moaned and, tearing her mouth away from his, threw her head back out of reach, exposing her long, delicate throat. "Please . . . don't."

"Why not? I have no effect on you," he rasped thickly while pressing warm, wet kisses along her throat. "I leave you totally cold, remember?" He sank his teeth into a sensitive spot on her bare shoulder, and a white-hot streak of pleasure-pain shot through her. "But what you do to me," he groaned. Then, pausing only to lick the sweet hurt away, he resumed his tantalizing trip down her shoulder to the scoop neckline of her gypsy blouse, which he traced with achingly tender kisses.

Arden's cry of protest came out a husky moan and her body arched involuntarily like a cat's.

"Yes!" he cried fiercely as his hands moved hungrily from around her back to caress her breasts.

"Don't," she said, gasping, but her own body

made a liar out of her as her thighs gripped his convulsively. The way she was straddling him, she could feel the proof of his desire right through the scratchy denim of his jeans, pressing hard against the soft exposed flesh of her inner thigh.

The shudder that went through her was almost frightening in its intensity, making it impossible for her to defend herself against the exquisite sensation of his tongue on her skin or the drugging warmth his fingers trailed softly along the curve of her breasts, or the intoxicating feel and smell of his balsam-sweet hair as it brushed against her skin. Overwhelmed by a barrage of emotions and sensations she'd never felt and didn't know how to handle, Arden struggled to recover her usual self-control. It was like swimming against a powerful current in slow motion.

"So soft . . . so soft and warm," she heard him gasp with wonder as if that were something *he'd* never known. "Sweet . . . vulnerable . . . delicious lady," he moaned, retracing his way up to her face with tiny nips and kisses, "where have you been all my life?"

His teasing smile tried to make light of what he'd said but he couldn't hide the naked yearning in his smoked silver eyes or the very real hunger in his kiss—a hunger that seemed more than just physical. She couldn't fight this, she realized in panic, there was no way she could fight this, but she had to.

She pressed frantic hands against his shoulders to push him away but they grabbed onto him instead, so hard that her nails dug into the taut muscles straining against his silk shirt. The shudder that shook his whole body went through hers as well and the moan deep in her throat echoed his. His arms locked around her, crushing her to him, and she found herself returning his kiss with every part of her.

He came out of the kiss as if he were coming up for air out of a deep dive: dazed, gasping for breath, a diver who'd gone beyond his depth. She could feel his hands shaking as they moved down her back, shaking as much as she was. They tightened suddenly around her waist and he slid her off him with an abrupt, almost angry motion.

"You can get out now," he muttered between clenched teeth.

"What?" she stammered uncomprehendingly.

Turning away from her, he bent down to retrieve her shawl, which had fallen onto the carpeted floor of the car. He tossed it into her lap.

"You can get out," he repeated evenly, nodding in the direction of the tinted window, and Arden realized with a shock that the Rolls was idling at the curb in front of her hotel.

She pulled the shawl around herself in a purely reflex action but continued staring at him blankly even though he kept his face hidden from her.

"Don't worry. I promise I won't sue you," he assured her sarcastically as he deliberately pushed a button and the car door swung open. "Your methods, though not very original, are very persuasive."

Arden gasped but no sound came out. Still totally vulnerable, she felt as though he'd slapped her. The blood drained from her face, leaving her deathly pale.

"You . . . all right," she heard him stammer, "listen, I . . ."

Arden stumbled out of the car, pulling the shawl tightly around her as if to hold herself together till she got inside, and ran blindly over to the entrance so he wouldn't see the tears streaming down her face.

4

Arden dragged herself out of bed the next morning, her eyes swollen, her nerves raw from the restless, dream-filled night. Before she even brushed her teeth, she called the airline office to change her reservation on a flight leaving the next evening to the first available flight back to New York. That meant she had less than two hours to pack, dress, and get to the airport, but she refused to remain in Miami one minute longer than she had to. She was determined to get away from Flint Masters as soon as possible.

But even as she rushed around collecting her things, trying to collect herself, she couldn't stop thinking about him. The events of the night before kept invading her mind, slowing her down. Her feelings about him were as jumbled as the clothes she tossed on the bed in her rush to pack. Just as she'd been unable to connect the bits and pieces she'd uncovered about him while researching the book, Arden now found it difficult to believe that the same man could be so passionately tender and so deliberately cruel and vindictive at the same time. She was even more amazed by the way she'd acted.

She thought she knew herself pretty well—until last night. Last night, Flint Masters had revealed a side of her she never knew existed. Arden had always prided herself on being self-possessed, especially where men were concerned. More than a few who'd tried to date her after Neil actually accused her of being aloof and unresponsive. Even Neil used to tease her about being shy and insecure sexually— though his kisses, she realized now, were far from earthshaking. If only those other men had seen her last night! It was a good thing Flint Masters stopped when he did or who knows what would have happened.

That disturbing realization propelled Arden over to the baggage rack for her suitcase, but she was interrupted by a knock on the door. Adjusting her robe to make sure it was closed properly, since she had on only a lacy bra and matching panties underneath, she released the latch to let the maid in with her clean laundry. Flint Masters was standing there instead, smiling down at her sardonically. Arden froze, clutching the top of her robe automatically. Before she could recover enough to slam the partially open door in his face, he was already easing his way through it.

"May I come in?" he asked drily.

Arden jumped back to avoid contact with his body but that only gave him the space he needed to enter.

"No! No, you can't come in here," she insisted angrily as he was already striding confidently into the room. "If you don't leave this minute, I'll call down to the desk and . . ."

"I'm already late for an important meeting," he interrupted impatiently as if *she* were the one who'd barged into his hotel room, "so I'll get right to the point. I'm here to offer you a job."

On her way over to the phone, Arden stopped to stare at him, wordlessly. It wasn't just the absurdity of what he'd said but the cold, impersonal tone of his voice. It implied that they were total strangers, that last night had never happened. She had to look at him to make sure he was the same man who'd made love to her only hours ago.

Everything about him was different this morning. Instead of casual clothes, he was wearing a custom-made, three-piece suit in a shade of charcoal as dark and severe as his eyes. The European styling made him look slimmer, surprisingly elegant, but couldn't completely hide the rugged, virile look of him that she remembered. A custom-tailored white shirt was left open at the collar, exposing his powerful neck, and a maroon tie dangled out of his jacket pocket like a silk noose. His thick black hair, with its startling shock of white slashing through it, was carefully groomed. He looked even more devastating than she remembered.

Arden was suddenly conscious of how dreadful she looked with her swollen eyes and pale, drawn face. She'd tied her hair carelessly on top of her head when she had taken a shower and clusters of still-damp curls tumbled all around her face. Her blue flannel robe, a going-away-to-school present from her favorite aunt, was as comfortable as an old shoe—and about as glamorous. On top of every-thing else, she was now furious with him for catching her looking like this. Since he obviously had no intention of leaving, she continued resolutely over to the telephone.

"I don't want to do this," she said coldly, "but if you don't leave, I'll . . . I'll have them throw you out."

He broke into a slow, mocking grin that seemed to dare her to try it.

She picked up the receiver. "I mean it," she warned.

"Then you'd better tell them to send up three or four of their best men," he said evenly. It wasn't a boast, just a simple statement of fact, and Arden didn't doubt him for a second. She suddenly had visions of broken furniture and front-page headlines.

When she hesitated, he added wryly, "Aren't you interested in my job offer?"

"Of all the gall!" She slammed the receiver down so hard that the bell jangled. "Do you actually believe . . . after last night . . . that I would work for you? That I would so much as . . . talk to you ever again?"

"But you *are* talking to me, and when you hear my offer, I'm sure you're going to work for me, too."

"Even *you* don't have that much money!" Arden snapped contemptuously.

"I know that," he admitted, with a look of obvious respect which threw her completely. "That's why I'm offering *you* this job. I want you to write my authorized biography."

"What?"

"I'm tired of people inventing stories about me. I realize now, thanks to you, that it's partly my fault because I've always refused to tell the true story. Well . . ." He sighed heavily. The decision, obviously, hadn't been an easy one. "Now, I'm ready to set the record straight."

He waited for her to say something but, once again, he'd succeeded in confusing her so thoroughly that she was unable to respond.

"Listen," he continued, with a quick glance at his watch, "I *really* am late for an appointment. Are you free tonight?"

"Tonight? Uhhh . . ."

"Let's have dinner so we can discuss this some more, OK?" He started for the door before she had a chance to answer. "I'll pick you up at eight."

"Hey, wait a minute!" Arden called out as he was closing the door behind him. "I don't believe this," she wailed. Less than an hour before she had changed her reservation because she didn't want to be in the same city with him!

Reaching the door in a few quick steps, she pulled it open forcefully. But he must have heard her call out to him, after all, because he was coming back in, and she crashed right into him.

The feeling of his body against hers sent a shock of

electricity through her, flooding her mind with memories of the night before. Powerful hands went around her waist to steady her.

"Are you all right?" he murmured, his warm breath brushing her temple.

"No!" She pushed away from him so violently that the front of her robe pulled open. She heard his sharp intake of breath as his lips parted softly. His eyes followed the swell of her breasts hungrily, burning through the wispy lace of her bra before looking up at her with that smoky intensity of the night before.

"No, I . . . I'm not free tonight!" Tugging her robe closed, Arden backed into the room. "If you'd given me half a chance I'd have told you that," she added angrily as she tightened her belt with shaking hands. "I won't have dinner with you and I don't want your job either!"

The smoldering intensity went out of his eyes, and his manner turned cold and impersonal again. Arden couldn't decide which bothered her more.

"Don't you think we should at least discuss it?" he asked as if she were a business prospect holding out for a better deal. He took a determined step back into the room.

"I . . . I thought you said you were late for an appointment." She staggered back several steps, then caught herself and stood her ground. "Or was that just another one of your tricks?" she added contemptuously.

Flint stiffened automatically. He was clearly a man who never allowed anyone to speak to him that way.

She expected him to turn and walk proudly out the door without so much as another word or look at her.

"My appointment will just have to wait," he said instead, as if he understood why she was acting that way—which infuriated her even more, because *she* didn't.

"Well, *I'm* late for an appointment, with a 707, that *can't* wait," she suddenly remembered, hurrying past him to the baggage rack. "So if you don't mind, I have to get ready now." She practically tore the valise off the rack.

Closing the door, Flint watched her lug it over to the bed. "I thought you were leaving tomorrow night."

Arden wasn't about to give him the satisfaction of asking how he found that out, especially since he didn't sound surprised by her change of plans, only vaguely curious. She concentrated on packing. Maybe if she ignored him, he'd go away; if not, she'd be leaving soon enough.

"Running away?" The mocking tone of his voice pulled her up short, made her realize that she was packing as frantically as if an invading army were at the gates of the city.

"I'm going home one day earlier than planned. What's so unusual about that?"

"You walked out on the big press conference and luncheon to do it," he said, continuing over to the bed. "I understand poor, dear Felicia is furious because you refused to back her up." He moved several of her filmy nightgowns to one side to make room for himself and sat down at the foot of the bed, making it impossible for her to ignore his disturbing presence.

"You sure look like you're running for your life." He smiled as he watched her tossing her jumbled clothes into the suitcase without even bothering to fold them properly. "What are you so afraid of?"

"I'm not afraid of anything!"

"Why else would you turn down such a fantastic offer?"

"My, don't we think we're something."

"No, I don't. But, for some reason, there are plenty of media people who do. I never could figure out why, myself." He shrugged as his hand casually traced the pattern of pink lace rosebuds that made up the bodice of her prettiest and most daring nightgown. "I'm sure I don't have to tell you that every publishing house in the country will be fighting for the rights to my story. Or what writing it would mean to your career."

There was something mesmerizing in the husky drawl of his voice and in the way his hand was smoothing out the folds of the nightgown with a slow, caressing motion. Arden suddenly re-experienced the sensation of his strong, warm hands on her skin.

Reaching abruptly for the nightgown, she pulled it away from him. "Do you mind?"

"It's lovely," he murmured, making her feel that he knew exactly how she looked in it.

Tossing the nightgown into the valise, she proceeded to bury it under still more clothes. "I'm not interested."

"Maybe I didn't make myself clear," he insisted. "I'm not asking you to ghostwrite . . . like the last one. This will be *your* book. *Your* name will be on it." He leaned towards her. "That's what you've always dreamed of, isn't it?"

Arden stopped her manic packing. She couldn't understand how he knew so much about her, right down to the dream that had sustained her through the lonely years of her childhood. And she felt, instinctively, that he was deliberately using that knowledge for some purpose of his own.

"Isn't it?" he demanded impatiently when she still hadn't answered.

"Yes!"

"Then what's the problem?"

"Why me?" She looked over at him, facing him squarely for the first time. "Why would you want *me* to write this book? Especially after the awful things you said about me last night?"

"Because I know now that I was . . . wrong about you," he admitted grudgingly, "and I guess I acted . . . pretty damn badly because of it. But I thought you were just another greedy little schemer like Felicia or . . ." He stopped himself, having obviously said more than he'd intended. Arden suddenly realized what it cost him to be saying this.

"Anyway"—he shrugged while brushing invisible lint off his trousers—"I checked up on your story, about the phone calls, and everything you said was true." A strange smile curved his lips as if he still had difficulty believing that. "Seems my secretary, knowing how I feel about my privacy, took it upon herself not to bother me with your messages." Rising impulsively, he took several awkward steps towards her. "I guess what I'm trying to say is . . . I'm sorry for the way I behaved last night."

"It's all right." Arden backed away from him, from the naked pleading in his voice and eyes. "I understand."

"You're all right, lady." His now-silvery eyes glowed and his smile was so warm and radiant that Arden was blinded by him. "One more thing." He closed the distance she'd put between them. "I want it understood that I apologize only for being so damn rude and for throwing you out of the car. Especially for throwing you out of the car." He laughed at the memory of it, a deep, sexy laugh that sent chills up her back. "But not for what else happened. No way could I ever say I'm sorry about that," he vowed intensely, and the whole experience came alive between them. Arden felt herself being drawn to him as if he had her on an invisible string.

"*You're* not sorry, are you?" he pleaded softly as he moved still closer, so close that she could smell the balsam in his hair, the scent of his skin. She realized that he was about to kiss her and that if he did she wouldn't be able to stop him.

Forcing herself to turn away from him, Arden reached blindly for the top of the suitcase. "I've got a plane to catch."

"You're not going to make *that* plane," he blurted out with obvious satisfaction.

"What?" A glance at her watch proved him right. She spun around in time to catch the victorious look on his face before he was able to suppress it and Arden felt tricked.

"But you've got plenty of time to make my plane," he said before she could recover. "I guess now I'll be flying home as originally planned . . . right after the meeting." He checked his watch impatiently. "That is, if there still is a meeting. I've really got to get going." His manner was polite but impersonal again, and Arden found herself watching him with growing fascination. "I'll send Albert to pick you up around four o'clock," he tossed over his shoulder at her as he started for the door.

"I don't believe this!" She burst out laughing. "You're . . . unbelievable!"

He turned back. "What do you mean?"

"No wonder you were rich and famous before you were thirty. You are some operator!"

"I don't understand," he said, all innocence.

"You actually expect me to go away with you . . . and stay with you at your place?"

"Why not?" he asked, perplexed. "What better way is there for you to research the book firsthand? You'll be able to see how I live . . . interview the people who work or live there with me. You'll have complete access to all my private lettters and diaries." He paused as if another thought had just occurred to him. "You don't think I'm inviting you to be a guest in my house for . . . some other reason, do you?"

"No . . . of course not." She felt like such a complete and utter fool now that she could have strangled him with her bare hands.

"I thought you wanted to know all there is to know about me."

"What?"

"For the book," he was quick to explain, but Arden sensed a double meaning in his words, a hint of sarcasm, yet she wasn't sure. She wasn't sure about anything with him!

"But I never agreed to write your damn book!" she exploded in total frustration.

"Of course you'll write the book." He shrugged confidently. "Give me one good reason why you shouldn't."

"Because I feel as though you're . . . kidnapping me again, like last night, and I resent it!"

"That's not the reason and you know it," he said with an ironic smile that again made her want to strangle him. Especially since she knew he was right. She couldn't give him a reason—at least not a sensible, intelligent one.

Arden stormed over to the window as if she were at the end of her patience, but actually she needed to get away from him in order to think clearly.

She couldn't shake the feeling that this was part of some plan of his, that he was deliberately setting her up to knock her down, as he did the night before. She couldn't understand why . . . unless he was still determined to pay her back for Felicia's book. Still, she fully realized that writing his biography would be the turning point in her career. It would also be a chance to finally unravel the puzzle of Flint Masters to her complete satisfaction, which somehow tempted her even more.

"So what's the verdict?" His query cut through her thoughts, forcing Arden to make a decision.

"It's a deal," she said, assuming an assurance she

didn't feel as she walked back over to him. "But, on two conditions."

"Which are?"

"One, this will be a strictly business arrangement. There will be no repetition of . . . of what happened last night."

He smiled. "That depends as much on you as it does on me, doesn't it?"

"And number two," she continued, refusing to let him rattle her, "there's to be no censorship. I'm to have final say over the material."

"No censorship, absolutely," Flint agreed in his business-executive voice. "I'll have my lawyer draw up a letter of agreement to that effect." He checked his watch impatiently. "I really have to go. I just hope the shipping tycoon I'm meeting with doesn't drive as hard a bargain as you do," he said on his way out.

From the doorway, Arden watched him striding down the hall in that powerful yet graceful way of his. He filled the space around him with such vibrant life that the hallway seemed narrower and not quite as high as she remembered. She realized, with a start, that he never did agree to her first condition, and she suddenly had the feeling that she was about to make the biggest mistake of her life.

Arden closed the door to shut out the disturbing sight of him, so she couldn't have seen the victorious gleam in his eyes as he waited for the elevator, or the slow, confident grin of a hunter who knows he's successfully baited the trap and has only to wait for it to snap shut.

5

Abandon hope, all ye who enter here," Arden quoted half-jokingly to herself as she boarded Flint Masters's seaplane later that afternoon.

She still had strong doubts about the whole affair —writing assignment, she rewrote her thoughts while struggling with the safety belt—but her determination to find the missing pieces of the puzzle called Flint Masters was even stronger. Yet, as she watched the mainland receding farther and farther into the distance, she felt as alone and vulnerable as the light aircraft suspended between the vast blue emptiness of sky and sea.

The flight to Lighthouse Key, Flint Masters's island home, turned out to be short and uneventful. Except for a polite "Welcome aboard," Flint ignored Arden completely and spent the entire trip feeding instructions into a portable computer the size of an attaché case, which rested easily on his powerful thighs.

Arden decided that he obviously meant to honor her first condition and was annoyed to find that she wasn't as happy about that as she thought she would be. She passed the time working out a rough outline of the book or jotting down her bird's-eye-view impressions of the Florida Keys. Curving southwards for a hundred miles, the islands looked like a string of emeralds embedded in a giant scimitar floating on a sun-dazzled sea. At the sight of them, Arden was unable to suppress an intense feeling of excitement. She wondered which island was his, and what surprises it would hold for her.

Her first surprise was already waiting—a stunning-looking blonde in her early twenties who greeted Flint when they arrived on his island.

"Sugar, what took you so long?" she called out in a little-girl-lost voice while moving down the red-wood deck surrounding the ultramodern villa with the experienced flair of a model on a runway. From the way she literally threw herself at Flint when she reached him, Arden guessed that she was Felicia's successor.

Though her coloring was different—she had platinum hair which fell straight to her bare shoulders and eyes the color and slant of a Siamese cat's—she had the same look as Felicia. She had the same delicate, high-fashion model's features, the same tall, willowy figure, all legs. She also shared Felicia's taste in designers. The strapless silk jersey gown she wore, which matched the color of her eyes and set off her golden tan to perfection, had Halston written all over it. She carried her beauty with the assurance of those blessed by the gods; she saw it as a magic key that would open doors forever closed to lesser mortals.

A lesser mortal was exactly what Arden felt herself to be in her simple, cream-colored blouse and slacks. Even worse, she felt downright invisible, as she stood awkwardly to one side while the stunning blonde carried on with Flint as if they were alone.

"I was starting to get worried," she said in her breathy, little-girl voice, tightening her hold on him.

Flint smiled indulgently while extricating himself from her possessive embrace. "We're not that late."

"If *you* were the one waiting, you'd think it was late." She pouted prettily. "Didn't you miss me?"

"Exactly as much as you missed me, I'm sure, Gayle," he muttered, adjusting his white linen sports coat.

Arden was shocked by the cutting sarcasm in his tone, even though it seemed completely lost on Gayle. So this is the way he treats a woman who loves him, she noted bitterly; it was just what she'd expected. She felt sorry for any woman dumb enough to fall in love with him, as she now felt sorry for Gayle. It was painfully obvious how happy she was to see him. Her face glowed with the excitement of a child's at Christmas.

"Where is it?" She laughed expectantly.

"Not now, Gayle," Flint muttered curtly, moving ahead of her onto the redwood deck. She rushed after him, refusing to be put off.

Still feeling like the invisible woman, Arden followed close behind, studying both of them carefully. She told herself she was only doing this as part of her research for the book, but she couldn't explain away the strange twinge of jealousy she felt as she watched Gayle running her bejeweled fingers over Flint's body.

"Come on, where is it?" she wheedled seductively. "Where are you hiding it?"

"What?"

"My present, silly." She giggled, going through his pockets playfully. "Where's my present?"

"I was too busy this trip to go shopping," Flint muttered impatiently with a quick backward glance at Arden.

Arden suddenly had the feeling that Flint wasn't as annoyed by the way Gayle was acting—it seemed to be a game they'd played before—as by her being a witness to it. She sensed the reason for his sarcasm now and couldn't help wondering if she'd been feeling sorry for the wrong person.

"I'll make it up to you the next time," he promised drily, having finally succeeded in getting her hands out of his pockets. "OK?"

Gayle pouted prettily again, and with a practiced toss of her head, which sent her platinum hair fanning out most attractively, suddenly turned her attention to Arden as if she were only now aware of her presence. Arden found herself being thoroughly inspected. From the accusing look in those ice blue eyes, she was sure Gayle suspected *her* of being the reason Flint was too busy this trip.

What happened between them in the Rolls flashed in her mind, burned on her face as Arden stood there self-consciously, hoping someone would put an end to the most awkward silence she'd ever experienced. Only by reminding herself that she'd never meant for it to happen, and that it was never going to happen again, did she manage to regain her composure.

"Hi, I'm Arden Stuart," she volunteered, since the perverse Mr. Masters was too busy enjoying this embarrassing little scene to make the proper introductions.

"Gayle Huntley," she allowed coolly, while continuing to appraise every feature of Arden's face, every curve of her body, with the knowing eye of a professional.

"I'm here on a writing assignment for Mr. Masters," she announced loud and clear, maybe a bit too loud, but she wanted to make sure everyone knew or remembered why she was there. Out of the corner of her eye, she caught the wry smile that curved Flint's mouth just before she offered her hand to Gayle.

Gayle raised a perfectly manicured hand, only to use it to smooth her smoother-than-silk hair before running it down her body. Obviously reassured, either by the feel of the expensive designer gown or by the exquisite shape it draped, she then took Arden's hand, dismissing her as no competition. Turning back to Flint with a sex-kitten smile, she purred seductively, "I've got something for you."

"What could that be, I wonder?" he asked cynically while continuing over to the entrance.

"I'll give you a hint." She smiled suggestively, "It's something you like a lot . . . and I do better than anybody else."

"Spend money?" Flint teased.

"No, silly, it's a piña colada. I did it just the way you like it." She giggled, grabbing onto Flint possessively. "Do you like piña coladas, Miss Steward?" she tossed over her perfumed shoulder as she all but dragged him into the house.

Ms. Stuart decided then and there that she hated piña coladas.

Flint Masters's ultramodern villa, all gleaming glass and burnished redwood, looked down from the highest elevation of the island over the tropical profusion of plants and flowers tumbling over one another on their way down to a narrow strip of beach. The seaplane, a gleaming white yacht, and several catamarans with multicolored sails nestled side by side in a sparkling cove. At the tip of the key, an old lighthouse rose starkly out of the rocks it seemed carved from. Lapped by a surfless, transparent sea, crowned by a cobalt blue sky, it hung in space, framed by the picture window of Arden's bedroom.

The room Arden had been assigned echoed the ultramodern look of the villa and was almost as large as the entire apartment she shared with two other girls in New York. The tiny alcove she was used to sleeping in would easily have fit into the walk-in closet, which seemed even bigger after Arden hung what she laughingly referred to as her wardrobe in it.

An interior decorator's hand was evident in the carefully selected and arranged furnishings, which were obviously expensive, yet tasteful. The color scheme was lime green and white, giving the room a bright, cool look—a little too cool for her taste, Arden decided. It was the kind of room you wouldn't dare leave your clothes lying around in.

She had the same feeling about the rest of the house. As she wandered from room to room the next day, making copious notes, Arden felt as if she were walking through a photo layout in *House Beautiful*. Somehow she couldn't connect any of it with Flint Masters. In spite of her somewhat negative feelings about him, she had to admit that he was an intensely alive man with a powerful and unique personality. None of that was reflected in his home. She studied every piece of furniture, every objet d'art as carefully as a detective searching out clues, but she couldn't find a trace of him anywhere.

Certainly not at dinner that first evening. If she were expecting to discover more about him through the company he kept, she was disappointed. All she discovered was just how invisible he could make himself when he wanted to.

Flint Masters could be called many things, she was sure, but phony wasn't one of them. Yet the glittering hangers-on he surrounded himself with couldn't be called anything else. All flash, no substance, they were the type usually found hanging out in fashionable restaurants and discos, hoping to get in with the "in" crowd. All they had was youth and beauty and a desperate willingness to do anything for a taste of the "good life." They reminded Arden of that Oscar Wilde character who knew the price of everything and the value of nothing.

Flint was a self-made man who had struggled against great odds to achieve everything he had, and Arden sensed an underlying contempt behind his perfect-host facade. Since he clearly had no illusions about his guests and refused to take part in their clever little games and bitchy conversation, Arden decided that he must be indulging Gayle, since they were obviously her friends. Several times during dinner, she caught him looking at her with the strangest smile, as if he could read every thought in her head. Once again, she had the scary feeling that this was all part of some plan of his.

The thick stone wall, which edged the sprawling deck at the back of the villa, seemed to Arden to mark a frontier between the ultracivilized world of the glass-and-redwood structure and the uncontainable profusion of nature that dominated the other side. The wall was high enough to keep a careless guest from tumbling down the hill but not so high that it spoiled the breathtaking view of the cove, and it was wide enough for Arden to rest her open notebook on.

The moon was a pale, thin sliver, but she was able to get enough light to write by from the multicolored Japanese lanterns strung all along the curved pool. She would have been able to see better and would have been far more comfortable on one of the many lounge chairs by the pool but she needed to get as far away from everyone as possible after that dinner. The wall was as far away as she could get. As it was, the sound of sophisticated banter being exchanged over after-dinner drinks drifted through the open windows. It clashed with the murmured rustling of banyan leaves and the softly insistent cry of a lonely night bird piercing the stillness at regular intervals. Because it had rained heavily, though briefly, during dinner, the heady smell of wet earth mingling with jasmine floated over the wall on a languorous breeze.

Normally, Arden would have been totally receptive to such new and exotic sensations, eager to capture them on paper, but her mind was still caught up with the events at dinner. She'd already made detailed notes on the food and service and the general ambience, but something vital was missing from her observations. She felt confused and disturbed by what she'd seen without knowing why.

She started jotting down vague impressions in an attempt to find the reason. Writing things down always helped her to understand them. Somehow it gave the confusion of life, the sometimes incomprehensible motives of other people, clarity and meaning for her.

"On the job already?" a deep, raspy voice inquired from behind, startling Arden out of her total concentration. She spun around with a tiny gasp that caught in her throat at the sight of him.

His darkly elegant evening clothes toned down but couldn't quite disguise his rugged build or the intense sexuality he projected so effortlessly. He'd removed his tie since dinner, and his silk shirt was casually open at the neck. Its stark whiteness intensified the deep copper tone of his skin and highlighted the white streak slashing through his thick, blue-black hair. A wry smile lingered on his mouth and his silver eyes were mocking.

Never in her life had Arden been so aware of a man physically. She turned back to the safety of her notebook. "I was just jotting down a few impressions."

"I thought it was understood that we were taking the weekend off." Flint stepped surely into her field of vision again. "Just couldn't wait to get started, I see," he muttered sarcastically, glaring at the notebook as if it were an instrument of blackmail.

"It's important to write things down while they're still fresh. Our memory has a way of altering the facts . . . even a day or two later." She flipped coolly to the next blank page, pleased with how thoroughly professional she sounded. She felt sure he didn't realize how much it bothered her to be alone with him. "This is still the best way to keep the facts straight."

"The facts?" He propped himself up against the wall directly in front of her, studying her with wry amusement while she scribbled away, ignoring him. "But life isn't made up just of facts," he insisted. "I believe most things are better . . . experienced than understood intellectually. Don't you?"

Arden hesitated for a moment because she sensed a double meaning in his words. He'd done this to her before, but she wasn't having any of it this time. "Not for a writer," she said pointedly. "A writer has to be objective."

"But there are some things that can't be explained

objectively. Like the chemistry between a man and a woman, for instance. That just can't be understood intellectually. Don't you agree?" He leaned towards her as if eager for her opinion, casting a shadow over the notebook, and Arden caught the scent of balsam in his hair. It was only a whiff, but for her it suddenly overpowered even the smell of wet earth and jasmine.

She straightened up, tugging at her dress as if that were the reason for her abrupt move. She regretted it instantly because of the way his eyes swept hungrily over her body.

"And even if it could," he smiled suggestively, "it still wouldn't change anything." He seemed so sure of himself, of his argument as well as his undeniable ability to charm even the wariest of females.

Something in her hardened against him. "I prefer to stick to the facts," she said coldly.

"Sounds very . . . sensible," he teased, "but one woman's fact may be another man's fancy. Take that dress you're wearing, for example." His silvery gaze skimmed casually over her plum silk dress this time. Casually, but thoroughly.

Just as she'd never been so aware of a man physically, he had a way of making her aware of her own body that was new and disturbing. She'd never realized how closely the bias-cut fabric molded her breasts or how it hugged the rounded line of her hips before falling in a swirl of loose pleats.

"What's wrong with my dress?" she snapped defensively.

"Absolutely nothing, believe me." He smiled appreciatively. "But *you'd* probably call that dress a fact—so much yardage, a specific fabric and color—but put that same dress on ten different women and you'd have ten different dresses. On most of those women you wouldn't even notice it. Yet on that one . . . particular woman, you wouldn't be able to notice anything else."

"That's an interesting theory," Arden said evenly. And one she was willing to bet worked every time. Especially when accompanied by a smile so appealing it just had to have been tried and tested. "No doubt the result of your vast experience with . . . women's fashions," she added lightly, trying to prove that she could play games too if she set her mind to it.

"Hardly. The only thing I know about women's fashions is the price tag."

"Oh?" He certainly could be honest, brutally so, when he wanted to. "So you must be an expert on women then?"

"No man is an expert on women." He laughed with a trace of bitterness. "Just when you think you know all there is to know about them . . ." He paused, smoky eyes searching her face intently. "Someone comes along to wreck all your preconceived notions."

Arden reached for her notebook again. "Can I quote you on that?" she asked flippantly, then spoiled it all by dropping her pen.

She bent down to pick it up but he was there ahead of her. His hand brushed hers and when she pulled back as though she'd been stung, he retrieved the pen. He offered it to her as if it were a weapon she'd been using against him, one that he was reluctant to return to her.

"Lady, you can quote . . . you can even misquote me," he teased, but the message in his eyes was serious. Arden grabbed the pen and he used it to pull her closer to him, so close that she could feel his warm breath brushing her lips. "You can do absolutely anything you want with me."

"Can I get you to stop fooling around long enough to give me an in-depth interview?" she asked coolly because she knew that he was about to kiss her and that she wouldn't be able to stop him.

"An interview?" His head pulled back sharply and she felt the tension go out of his hand, making it easy for her to pull the pen away. Getting to her feet took more of an effort because her legs were shaking. As Arden was fumbling the pen back into its cap, which was hooked firmly onto her notebook cover, she felt him rising slowly behind her.

She was grateful for the burst of laughter pouring through the open windows. She wasn't sure whether it had been going on all along or if she was only aware of it now because of the tense silence between them. She turned towards the villa as if she were actually interested in what was going on. She had no trouble making out Gayle's lithe figure. Some kind of parlor game seemed to be in progress, probably charades.

More games, she thought irritably as she started gathering up her notebook while Flint watched her with disappointment in his eyes. When it came to playing games, she knew she wasn't even in his league. He had more moves than a chess master. He even had her wondering whether he was playing a game with her or not!

"An interview?" he repeated drily while Arden stuffed her notebook back into its compartment in her tote bag. He must have sensed that she was planning to take off because he stepped directly in front of her, blocking her escape route. "And here I was, offering you all of me." He sighed self-mockingly, trying to make a joke of it. "And all you want from me is an interview?"

A fresh burst of laughter floated on the breeze. Arden was sure she heard Gayle's breathless, little-girl giggle. "That's why I'm here," she reminded him firmly, "to write your biography, remember?"

Flint's attempt at a smile faded, and Arden saw something inside him pull back, shut down, before he looked away from her. When he turned back, it was with a typically derisive grin. "You know what's wrong with you?"

"No . . . but I'm sure you'll tell me."

"You seem to be a very together lady. Intelligent, sensitive, and self-sufficient; yet feminine. Physically, you're more desirable than any one woman has the right to be. But somewhere along the line you decided to observe life rather than live it."

"That's not . . . true," Arden muttered, almost to herself. It couldn't be true.

"I think it is. And it's a damn shame because I never met a lady with a . . . lustier appetite for life. Or one more afraid to admit it."

"That's ridiculous!" she protested angrily. The smug look on his face made it clear he knew he'd hit a nerve. "What do you know about me, anyway?"

"Only what I've . . . experienced," he murmured suggestively, forcing her to remember everything that happened between them the other night, everything she'd been trying so hard to forget. "And I know one more thing." He grinned. "You can write it all down in that little notebook of yours. You can work out some sensible, logical explanation for it all . . . but you still can't change what happened."

Before Arden could recover enough to find an appropriate comeback, Flint was already striding down the deck towards the villa. She watched him travel the length of the pool and step surely onto the patio before moving through the sliding glass doors.

"I don't believe this!" She laughed, though it came out in sharp, brittle pieces. She'd come here to uncover things about *him* . . . not the other way around. Still, she had to admit that some of what he'd said was true . . . maybe more than she'd care to admit. One thing was for sure: he was far more complex than she'd given him credit for, and every bit as devious. She was starting to believe that Flint Masters was like one of those ancient Chinese conundrums: a puzzle within a puzzle within a puzzle. She was determined to get through layer after layer until she uncovered the very core of him. She just had to make sure he didn't get to her first.

Flint proved true to his word about taking the weekend off. He spent most of it sailing with a couple of ancient ex-fisherman now in his employ. Authentic "conchs" from Key West with surprisingly wiry bodies, still piercingly alert eyes, and skins like burnished leather, they were living relics of a time in the keys which no longer existed except in Hemingway's novels.

The care and feeding of Flint's guests was left in Gayle's more-than-eager hands. Playing the role of society hostess to the hilt, she presided over an endless round of champagne brunches, cocktail parties, and seven-course dinners. In between, she kept the fun and games going with the relentless cheerfulness of an entertainment coordinator at a singles' resort.

Left stranded on the edge of things—not quite a guest, not really an employee—Arden was free to observe what was going on without being noticed. Unlike Gayle, she soon understood why Flint preferred the sea and the company of two simple but fascinating old men to her shallow friends. He let his guard down when he was with them, she noticed, revealing an outgoing, down-to-earth side of himself she'd never seen before and would never have expected. She had to admit that there was more to him than his much-publicized playboy image had led her to believe. She was starting to question some of her preconceived notions about him.

She often found herself lingering by the stone wall, out of range of the noisy partying which went on endlessly at poolside. She would drag one of the lounge chairs over there and laze for hours in the sun, watching the sleek, white lines of Flint's yacht as it sliced through the seamless blue of sky and water. Her notebook lay forgotten in her lap.

She told herself there was no point in interviewing

any more guests because, apparently, all they knew about Flint, or cared to know, was the extent of his hospitality. One person who seemed to know and care the most about him was Mrs. McNally, his housekeeper. A feisty but warm-hearted woman, she fussed over him like an old mother hen. Arden genuinely liked the woman, who seemed to return the feeling. But since Mrs. McNally guarded Flint's privacy as fiercely as he did, there was no point in interviewing her either. Besides, the sun was too hot, the view far too beautiful to allow her to concentrate on work. And, though she'd be the last one to admit it, she was really waiting for his return.

Whenever Flint came back from a sail, hair tousled by the wind, copper skin still glistening with sea spray as he bounded up the cobblestone path, he exuded a primitive kind of joy and satisfaction that made her feel strangely happy. It saddened her somehow to see it fade to a guarded expression once he stepped through the wrought-iron gate onto the sun deck. By dinner time, that sardonic mask of his was firmly in place.

Flint had made no further attempt at being alone with her since that first evening. If anything, he seemed to be going out of his way to avoid her. Yet she would catch him looking at her in the strangest way at times, as if he didn't quite know what to make of her and was trying to puzzle her out. Arden wasn't used to being at *that* end of the microscope. She assumed it was his perverse way of turning the tables on her, and it bothered her more than she showed or was willing to admit. She knew he must be comparing her to Gayle and the other women present. Since she refused to take part in the risqué jokes and meaningless flirtations which seemed to be their favorite pastime, she was sure he thought her hopelessly square.

All in all, it turned out to be quite a weekend for Arden. She couldn't remember ever being so fascinated, bored, confused, relaxed, irritated, or strangely happy. She wondered what was in store for her once they started working together.

6

~~~~~~~~~~~~~~~~

Except for a few live-in guests, everyone left the villa first thing Monday morning. Arden welcomed the change, delighting in the natural sounds and rhythms of the island. She'd had a restless night but was up earlier than usual and, instead of being tired, felt as energetic as a child on Christmas morning. She told herself she was excited because she was starting on a new book and found an equally logical explanation for the letdown that followed when Flint's secretary told her he'd gone to the mainland for a series of meetings. That meant he would not be available for the rest of the week. On his orders, the slim, almost frighteningly efficient Ms. Hardy deposited a stack of papers on Arden's desk, along with a copy of the letter of agreement, and an envelope containing a generous cash advance against sales. After Arden signed receipts for all of the above, Ms. Hardy extended her hand, a wary welcome, and a polite offer of assistance. Something in her tone bothered Arden. When she was alone again she realized what it was. Flint's secretary obviously had her own theory about Arden's reason for being there.

Arden spent most of the day sifting through the huge stack of papers, searching out the personal information he'd promised her, hoping to find some missing pieces of the puzzle. But the papers turned out to be mostly memos, letters, and press releases on Flint's various business coups. She found nothing that wasn't already part of the public record or that could even remotely be considered personal. By late afternoon, feeling thoroughly disgusted, she was reduced to typing up her own notes from the weekend. She was so involved that she didn't hear the knock on the door or realize someone had come in until Gayle was standing a few feet away from the desk.

Arden looked up, startled. "Oh, I . . . I didn't hear you come in."

"I knocked . . . twice," Gayle explained breathlessly. "I hope you don't mind."

"No, of course not."

"I was just too busy this weekend; we never had a chance to get to know each other." She smiled sweetly.

It was the first time in three days that Gayle had so much as acknowledged her existence, let alone smiled at her, and Arden hesitated for a moment. "It certainly is busy around here on weekends," she allowed finally, willing to give her the benefit of the doubt. "I'm glad you stopped by."

Arden really was glad for the chance to get to know Gayle better. The stunning blonde was, after all, one of the main pieces of the puzzle and she was intensely curious about her and her relationship with Flint—though she wasn't entirely sure whether what she felt was the curiosity of a writer or a woman.

"So how do you like your room?" Gayle's pale blue gaze swept over the room ever so casually, yet Arden had the feeling it didn't miss a thing. "Are you comfortable here?"

"Yes, thanks. Everything's lovely."

"This *is* one of the choicest suites," Gayle admitted drily before dismissing it with a toss of her platinum hair, "but you should see my place if you think this is something." She glided casually over to the huge brass bed. "I've got the penthouse. Flint let me redecorate it and everybody says it's a real showplace." She paused to check out the titles of several books which Arden kept on the night table. "You have to come up and see it."

"I'd love to."

"You'll have to take off your shoes . . . like in a Japanese restaurant." She laughed gaily as if reassured by what she'd found. "Because everything's white. The carpet, the furniture, the drapes . . . everything."

"It sounds lovely."

"I got the idea from a Lana Turner movie," she confided proudly as she walked back to the desk. She'd obviously gotten that walk from a Lana Turner movie also.

"So what are you doing?" she asked wonderingly, staring at the typewriter as if it were some kind of mechanical marvel she'd never seen before.

"Just working."

"Working?" she repeated incredulously as if that were totally foreign to her, too.

"Just typing up some notes and ideas for the book."

Bending over carefully, so as not to put an undue strain on the seams of her skintight, hot pink jump suit, Gayle peered over Arden's shoulder at the page in the typewriter as if she actually had to see it to believe it. "You mean, you're *really* going to write this . . . book?"

"Really." Arden sighed a bit impatiently. She was beginning to get tired of everyone doubting her. "That's why Mr. Masters invited me here."

A thoughtful frown disturbed Gayle's perfect features as she straightened up slowly. "But aren't you the one who wrote that other book? The one with . . . what's-her-name? The redhead?"

"Felicia Marlowe."

"That's right. Aren't you the one?"

"Guilty as charged," Arden murmured wryly.

"Boy, was Flint sore at you!" Gayle giggled like a mischievous little girl. "I've never seen him so mad."

"Yes, I know," Arden said, remembering. Just the thought of their first meeting was enough to send shivers up her back.

"So how come he asked *you* to write this book then?"

Arden was completely thrown for a moment. Not so much at the question, which she'd asked herself a few dozen times, but at the startling change in Gayle's manner. Her voice had lost that breathy "dumb blonde" quality, and the look she gave Arden was direct instead of coy.

"I suppose he realized that if he wanted the whole truth told, he'd have to tell it himself."

"So this . . . book was his idea then?"

"Yes. Completely."

Gayle turned and swayed her way back across the room. Arden couldn't see her face but she felt sure Gayle was upset about her being there. She knew how hurt and jealous she would be if she were in Gayle's place and thought Flint was interested in another woman. She had an impulse to reach out to Gayle, to assure her that she had nothing to worry about.

Arden pushed her reading glasses firmly against the bridge of her nose. If she were going to stay on and work with Flint she had to keep everything on a strictly business level, even her thoughts. She tore a page out of the typewriter and, crumpling it up, tossed it in the wastebasket.

"Do you have enough closet space for all your clothes?" Gayle was inquiring breathily as she slid the mirrored doors of the walk-in closet open.

"More than enough." Arden couldn't help smiling. "As you can see."

"Is that all you brought with you?" Gayle's bejeweled fingers picked through Arden's meager wardrobe. "I'd go through that in a week. How long were you planning on staying?"

"I'm not sure. A few weeks . . . a month. It all depends on the amount of research I have to do."

Her answer seemed to reassure Gayle because she broke into a dazzling smile. "You're going to need more clothes then. I go shopping every Tuesday and Thursday. Why don't you come along? I'm sure I can talk Flint into footing the bill."

"No! Thanks but . . ."

"Oh, wow!" Gayle exclaimed, obviously impressed with the black satin evening gown Arden had bought on sale at Bloomingdale's on an impulse but had never had occasion to wear. "A Valentino?" she asked on a mere wisp of a breath, her eyes glowing.

"God, no. It's just a copy of a copy."

"Oh." The tiny word held a world of disillusionment, like the look she shifted in Arden's direction. "You know something," she said finally, after inspecting every feature of Arden's scrubbed-clean face, her long golden hair tied up in a ponytail, and her well-worn jeans and plain cotton shirt, "you could be rather . . . attractive, if you just did something with yourself."

"Thanks, I think."

"No, I mean it. You should let *me* do you sometime. I'm a whiz with makeup. You know, we get lots of wealthy VIPs as guests here," she added confidentially, "and I'm sure some of Flint's older business associates might go for someone like you. You never know, you just might be able to hook one and you'd be set for life."

"I'm really not looking to . . . hook anyone,"

Arden said as pleasantly as she could manage. The idea of turning herself into bait to hook some poor, unsuspecting male had never appealed to her.

"But then you wouldn't have to work for a living, silly!"

"I like working for a living . . . and right now all I'm interested in is writing this book, so . . ."

"You really believe Flint's going to let you write this book?" Gayle said sharply, turning her attention back to Arden's wardrobe.

"Of course."

"Then you don't know Flint Masters. Not that anybody does . . . not even me and I'm . . . you know." Gayle paused to check the label in Arden's best silk dress. "But I know him well enough to know he's not going to let anybody write any book about him." She pushed the dress to one side as if the designer wasn't up to her standards. "Flint never gives himself away to anybody."

"I'm sure he's not that way with you." Somehow Arden couldn't believe he would be like that with someone he loved. "He must talk to *you* about himself."

"The last thing he wants to do when he's with me is . . . talk," Gayle purred suggestively. "Of course, I'm not smart like you. I don't read the kind of books you do or . . ."

"I get the impression, Gayle, that you're very smart."

"No, it's OK." She shrugged with obvious self-satisfaction. "I'd rather be like me. Men can't stand girls who are too smart. I'm sure Flint can't. He's more interested in other things." She paused to make sure Arden had gotten her point before turning back to sizing up her wardrobe. "But even when he does talk, it's never about anything personal. That's just how he is." She sighed disgustedly but Arden wasn't sure whether the sigh was a comment on the state of her wardrobe or on Gayle's relationship with Flint.

"I know most women wouldn't care for that, but it's what I like the most about him," she declared, sliding the mirrored doors closed. "He's not jealous or possessive like lots of other guys. He respects your space . . . so you can do your own thing." Gayle lingered in front of the mirrors as if held there by the power of her own reflection. "Though sometimes I wish he were a bit more . . . demonstrative," she added wistfully, "at least in front of other people." She smoothed out her already silky smooth hair and touched up the perfectly drawn line of her glossy mouth. "But I know he's crazy about me," the lovely image in the mirror assured her. "He's just not the wildly passionate type."

"He's not?" Arden blurted out, amazed. She thought he was the most intensely, almost frighteningly passionate man she'd ever met. "I mean, he certainly doesn't give that impression."

"Oh, don't misunderstand me . . . he's great in bed, it's just . . ." Gayle spun around from the mirror to face Arden.

Trying to hide the pained expression she was sure Gayle had seen on her face, Arden reached blindly for some typing paper.

"Oh, no you don't," Gayle said in a strong, hard voice, "you're not getting anything out of me you can put in that book. I'm not dumb like Felicia. I know a good thing when I've got one."

Arden looked back up at her, not bothering to hide the shock on her face this time.

"What I mean is," Gayle hastened to add breathily, "Flint's been very good to me, and I would never do anything that would make him mad."

"But I thought you said he has no intention of letting me write this book."

"That's . . . right," she murmured vaguely.

"Then why did he invite me here?"

"I'm sure *I* don't know." Gayle's baby blue eyes widened innocently. "I thought *you* would tell *me*."

7

~●●●●●●●●●●~

By the time Arden completed her hike down the cobblestone path from the villa to the narrow strip of beach, there was a single catamaran left out of all the ones that had been dotting the horizon. Sailing proudly into the wind, the stripes of its sail echoing the yellow-orange-red glow streaking the late-afternoon sky, it seemed determined to put off the end of such a perfect day for as long as possible. Reflecting the play of light and color, the sea lay as smooth as a mirror, untouched by the soft, jasmine-scented breeze.

At her approach, tiny sunbathing lizards scattered among the drooping ferns and magenta masses of bougainvillea which spilled over the edge of the beach. A tree frog dozing on a cool banana plant looked up at her, unconcerned, while from the depths of lush trees unseen birds called out to one another, piercing the stillness.

Feeling like Eve awakening to her first day in the Garden of Eden, Arden slid off her sandals and, digging her toes into sand the color of crushed pearls, removed her nylon wraparound. She dropped it languidly next to her beach bag, taking in a deep, refreshing breath of air, when something glimpsed out of the corner of her eye made her turn towards the lighthouse. Her breath caught in her throat as she saw Flint Masters striding down the jetty towards the beach.

It wasn't the surprise of seeing him that made her gasp, but the way he looked. Naked, except for the French-cut swimsuit which emphasized rather than hid his obvious masculinity, he looked as primitive as the lush surroundings. The reddish glow of the sun intensified the deep copper tone of his skin, high-lighting every muscle of his powerful but lithe body. His hair gleamed blue-black, matching the tangle of curls that tapered down his chest and disappeared under his swimsuit. He moved with the powerful grace and unconscious beauty of a wild stallion. Arden felt her mouth go dry, her pulse quicken. Never had she been so affected by the mere sight of a man. She kept staring at him, unable to look away.

Stepping off the jetty, he turned onto the beach and saw her for the first time. His look of surprise at her being there warmed into an impulsive smile of greeting before turning sardonic as he covered the distance between them in a few long-legged strides.

"What are you doing here?" he asked, his appreciative glance stripping her modest bathing suit from her.

Tiny dots dancing in front of her eyes as though she'd been staring at the sun too long, Arden dropped to one knee to hunch over her beach bag. "I thought I'd go for a swim before dinner."

"Why here?" Hunkering down next to her, he watched her tugging her beach towel out of the bag. "Why don't you use the pool like everyone else?"

"Because I want to go for a swim," she insisted, spreading out her towel with the grim determination usually reserved for the most demanding of tasks, "and lounging around a pool sipping piña coladas isn't my idea of swimming." She regretted the obvious dig at Gayle and her friends the instant she made it, but his mocking chuckle made her realize that he felt the same way. She gave him a long, thoughtful look. "Why aren't *you* using the pool like everybody else?" she asked pointedly.

"You don't usually swim here, do you?" He answered, typically, with another question, which Arden knew by now was his way of telling her it was none of her business.

"No, this is the first time."

"Don't ever swim here alone," he warned sternly. "It can be dangerous."

"I happen to be an excellent swimmer," Arden assured him proudly as she continued making a major project out of smoothing out the beach towel.

"After the breakers at Jones Beach, swimming in this surfless sea should be like taking a bath."

Going down on his knees, Flint grabbed her suddenly and slid her around to him, scraping her knees lightly on the sand. "I'm not joking," he muttered intensely. "That's a coral sea out there. Under that calm, enticing exterior lurk sudden depths and hidden dangers."

That's exactly how she felt about him, Arden thought ruefully, as she started to pull away. She was stopped by the look of genuine concern in his silvery eyes as he tightened his hold, drawing her closer until their half-naked bodies were only inches apart.

"Promise me you'll never swim here alone," he insisted. "Promise!"

"All right," Arden conceded just so he'd let go of her. Right now the blinding closeness of him, the feeling of his powerful hands on her bare skin held far more danger for her than any coral sea. "All right," she repeated, twisting nervously out of his grasp. "I promise." She turned her full attention back to the beach towel and was surprised and annoyed to find that her hands were trembling.

"You think you'll be through with that towel before the sun sets?" He laughed and Arden realized he knew she was using it as a way of not dealing with his disturbing presence.

She forced a cool smile, a careless shrug. "That's the best I can do with it."

"Looks good to me." Sprawling all over it, he grinned up at her astonished face. "Certainly was very nice of you to bring a beach towel big enough for the two of us." But, as ample as the towel was for her, it could barely contain him. He took up most of the width and his feet stuck out over the edge onto the sand when he stretched out full-length with a groan of undisguised pleasure.

She meant to protest his taking over her towel but something turned over inside her at the sight of him. She'd never realized a man's body could be so beautiful, or project such a natural, yet intense, sexuality. She felt a sudden crazy urge to run her hands all over his body, to cover him with kisses from head to foot. . . .

Arden reached for her beach bag and then started rummaging around inside it. Her hand found her reading glasses automatically, and she slid them on. The familiar feel of the cool metal frames helped her remember who she was and why she was there.

"Aren't you going to lie down?" Flint squinted up at her. "There's still over an hour of sun left."

"I just want to make a few notes first," she stated in her professional-interviewer voice, "about the coral sea."

"Ah, the famous notebook," he muttered sarcastically when she removed it from her bag. "You actually take it everywhere you go, don't you? I bet you even take it to bed."

Ignoring the implications of that statement, Arden flipped through to the next blank page.

"Am I right?" he needled playfully, but he couldn't disguise an underlying tone of bitterness which Arden was at a loss to understand. "Do you take it to bed with you?" he asked.

"Is that why there's a lighthouse on the island?" Arden answered, giving him a taste of his own medicine. "I wondered why one was needed when the sea's as smooth as glass."

"Coral reefs," he stated flatly. "Two hundred years ago, when pirates roamed freely here, the coral reefs were the only real threat to their safety. The skeletons of quite a few of their ships can still be found lying at the bottom. I'd be glad to show them to you . . . if you're into scuba diving." He rolled onto his side, propping himself up on one elbow. He was so close to her that his hair brushed against her arm. "This weekend if you want."

Arden was about to slide farther away from him but she was already sitting on the edge of the beach towel. "Pirates . . . how fascinating!" she said with just a bit too much enthusiasm. She continued scribbling furiously in her notebook as if she hadn't heard his offer; it had taken her by surprise and she couldn't decide what to do about it. "Is the lighthouse still in use? From my window at night I see lights on inside."

Flint hesitated for a moment. "Yes, it's still in use," he said evenly, lying down again. "But not as a working lighthouse. I've had it completely remodeled inside and that's where I live."

"Really?" Arden was so surprised that she stopped scribbling to look at him. She'd assumed he shared the penthouse at the villa with Gayle. "You actually live . . . in the lighthouse?"

"That's right."

"How fantastic," she exclaimed, but this time the emotion was genuine. "Imagine living in a lighthouse!"

Flint raised a wary eyebrow as if he couldn't

decide whether she was putting him on or not.
"Some people think that makes me a bit eccentric."
From the tone of his voice it was clear he didn't give
a damn what anyone thought.

"Eccentric . . . why?" Arden laughed with disbelief. "I'd call it . . . unique."

"You . . . would?"

"Yes." She looked over at the lighthouse jutting
proudly out of the rocks it seemed carved from. Now
she understood why she hadn't been able to find a
trace of him in the villa. *That's* where the missing
pieces of the puzzle were hidden. "I'd love to see the
inside of it." She couldn't have hidden the excitement in her voice even if she had wanted to, and it
glowed in her sapphire eyes when she turned back to
him. "When can I see it."

"You never stop, do you?" he muttered caustically.

"What do you mean?"

"Is that all you ever think about . . . that book?
Can't you ever forget it and just relax? I thought you
came down to the beach, like me, to get away from
everybody and have a quiet, relaxing swim."

"I was only trying to get to know you," Arden
protested, "and this is the first chance I've had
since . . ."

"I don't mind your trying to get to know me," he
cut her off angrily. "I would love for you to *really* get
to know me, but do you always have to make a
goddamn research project out of it?" Pulling himself
up abruptly, Flint hunched over his raised knees to
stare straight out at the raft anchored two hundred
yards from the beach.

Arden was stunned by his outburst. She felt sure it was just pride, yet she couldn't deny the undisguised hurt edging the anger in his voice. She stared wordlessly at his strong profile, the tiny vein beating violently in his jaw. She didn't know what to say. How could she tell him that the only way she could deal with him was in her usual rational manner, that she didn't dare relax with him? All she could say, finally, was, "I didn't mean it to seem that way . . . I'm sorry."

"It's no big deal." He shrugged, and when he turned back to her, it was with a typically sardonic smile. "If you *really* want to get to know me . . ." Reaching out, he ran a rough hand along her thigh. "I know a much better way."

The caress was a deliberately provocative one and it raised goose bumps, sent chills through her. A feeling of confused anger swept over her at this inexplicable change in him and at his being able to unnerve her so easily. She brushed his hand away as if it were a slightly annoying insect. She even managed a sardonic smile of her own. "When I said I wanted to know you, I didn't mean it in the biblical sense."

"What truer way is there for a man and a woman to get to know each other?" Starting at her toes, he drew a teasing finger slowly over her instep, up her raised calf, lingeringly back down the length of her thigh, the nail leaving a thin, white line and shivers behind. When it slid over her pelvic bone to start tracing the edge of her swimsuit, Arden pushed it away, angrily.

"Look," she said coldly, "I don't know why you

asked me here to write your biography when you refuse to cooperate. So far you haven't given me any help whatsoever, not one single scrap of personal information as you promised. If you never intended to keep the conditions you agreed to then why did you ask me here?"

A perverse little smile curved his mouth. "Why do you think I asked you here?"

"I don't know anymore!" Arden finally exploded in frustration. "But I know what Gayle thinks the reason is!"

Leaning back on his elbows, Flint stretched out again, squinting up into the sun as if trying to gauge its progress. "Gayle is much smarter than she pretends to be," he allowed drily. Before Arden could decipher the meaning of that cryptic remark, he added, "That dumb-blonde routine is just her way of getting everything she wants. Don't let it fool you."

She'd had that thought herself but coming from him it seemed rather cold-blooded. "That's not a very generous thing to say about someone you're . . . in love with."

"Where did you get that idea?" Cool silver eyes looked up into her startled ones.

"What?"

"That I'm in love with Gayle? She couldn't have told you that."

"Well, she certainly gives that impression. I'm sure *she* thinks you love her."

"Really?" He seemed amused by her naïveté. "I certainly never had any such illusions about her."

"Then why are you lovers?"

"Who said we're lovers?"

95

"Oh, come on now!" Just how naïve did he think she was?

"We sleep together, if that's what you mean. But that doesn't make us lovers." The cynical tone of his voice held a trace of bitterness. As if he were aware of it too, Flint turned his attention to the deepening colors of the sky over the horizon.

"I don't understand how . . ." Arden started to say before she reminded herself that not everyone had her medieval ideas about love and commitment which, even she had to admit, existed only in books these days.

"It's easy enough to understand. Gayle enjoys the kind of life I can offer, and through me she meets people who can advance her modeling career." A bemused look flickered in his eyes as he studied her reaction. "You find that shocking?"

"Not Gayle's reasons, no . . . but the way you accept that kind of relationship as though it were the most natural thing in the world. It's almost as though you don't believe she could be with you because she cares for you and not for purely selfish reasons."

"Everybody's out for himself," he stated flatly. "Some people are just more honest than others."

"You don't really believe that?"

"Aren't you writing all this down in your little notebook?" he replied sarcastically, turning onto his side and away from her searching look to peer over her raised leg at the empty page. "Just a moment ago you were complaining that I never tell you anything personal."

Now Arden almost wished he hadn't, because his revelation had confused and disturbed her. She was losing her professional objectivity, she realized. She felt touched, even saddened, by what he'd just revealed, yet strangely elated at the same time. "I think I'll go for a swim before it's too late." She started to close her notebook but Flint thrust a demanding hand on it, holding it open, pressing it down hard on the thigh on which it was resting.

"I insist you write down what I just said. It's a fact," he added pointedly, "and you're big on facts, remember? I want it down there in black and white so there's no chance you'll forget what I just told you."

Arden knew there was no way she could forget it . . . or its implications. She wished now that he hadn't told her about himself and Gayle and wondered why he had. She sighed with exasperation. "You're an impossible man!"

With a warm chuckle, Flint removed his hand from the notebook, relieving the pressure on her thigh. "You can put that down too, if you like."

"I don't have to write that down; I know it only too well!"

"I'm glad you know something about me," he teased. While Arden proceeded to make notes, he leaned in closer, glancing over her raised knee to make sure she was getting it right. The way he was lying next to her, propped up on one elbow, his head was level with her breast. The balsam-sweet scent of his hair was stirring up memories she'd tried hard to forget, making it almost impossible for her to concentrate.

"That's good," he approved when she'd finished, "now we can go for that swim."

"But that's only one side of it," Arden blurted out before she could stop herself, and she wasn't sure whether it was the writer or the woman speaking. "What about *your* reasons for being with Gayle?"

He seemed thrown for a moment—he was obviously used to people playing the game by his rules—but quickly recovered. "My reason for being with Gayle? Let's see . . ." He paused as if it were something he hadn't given much thought to. "Gayle's beautiful . . . even desirable . . . the perfect hostess," he went on, enunciating every word as though he were dictating a memo to his secretary, "and she's very . . . practiced in the art of making love."

Arden's pen hesitated for a fraction of a second but he picked up on it instantly.

"I'm not going too fast for you, am I?" He smiled that wicked smile of his, and if the pen were a knife, Arden would have gladly stuck it into his cold-blooded, irritating, aggravating heart!

"No problem." She smiled sweetly.

"Where was I?" he wondered, all innocence. "Ah, yes . . ." He used a muscular shoulder to prod her to keep on writing. "And she's *very* practiced in the art of making love," he repeated deliberately. Each word was like a tiny stab and Arden realized that *he* was the one holding the knife. He even gave it a final twist. "Technically, a most proficient lady."

"Well, seems to me you've got it made . . . no pun intended," she managed to joke but her voice was sharper than she'd meant it to be.

"That's what I thought too," he muttered, almost to himself, "but then I went for a ride in a Rolls."

Arden tensed visibly. She could put up with his sarcasm, but not about that night. The feelings she'd exposed went too deep to be made fun of.

"That's when I found out that no amount of expertise can compare with real passion," he said to the beach towel, "and what it's like to feel someone shaking all over when you kiss her." He looked up at her then, silvery eyes full of that intense longing she'd seen only once but which still haunted her dreams. "You've wrecked me for anybody else, lady, you know that?" It sounded like an accusation.

Reaching up suddenly, Flint slid the glasses off her face. Astonished, Arden felt as naked as if he'd just removed her most intimate garment. Dropping her glasses in the beach bag, he reached up again to dig his fingers into the soft coil of hair at the back of her head, drawing her face down to his. "I haven't been able to see anyone else since."

"But there is someone else," Arden reminded him with a gasp, breaking the sensuous spell he'd almost caught her up in. She twisted her head, trying to break his physical hold as well, but he tightened his grip as if afraid to let go of her.

"No, there isn't. That's what I just tried to tell you."

"I don't care what you told me! All I know is that Gayle is waiting for you by the pool, as she does every evening . . . all decked out and . . ."

"She doesn't do that for me!"

". . . and with your piña colada!"

"I don't give a damn about piña coladas." He laughed drily. "Not since I tasted Pernod." He moved to "taste" it again but Arden pushed him away with all her strength. Since most of his weight was resting on one elbow, he went sprawling on his back. Her pen and notebook went flying also as she jumped up and ran towards the water.

She heard him call out a warning, which she ignored. He called out to her again as he came after her; then, obviously annoyed by her stubborn independence, stopped ankle-deep in the water and glared at her silently. Arden kept skipping through the warm shallows, when the bottom suddenly dropped away. Caught unawares, she went under.

Fighting the first moment of panic, she managed to find her balance and was about to work her way back to the surface when she glimpsed the enticing beauty of the coral reef gleaming like a mirage beneath her. Kicking her feet expertly, she plunged deeper into the sea, eager for a closer look at the extraordinary world shimmering just out of reach. Suddenly a huge, dark shape from out of nowhere knifed through the water just above her head. She froze, her eyes shutting automatically against the vision of huge jaws opening up to devour her; gasping instinctively for air, she swallowed water. Choking, she tried to cough it back up but swallowed more water instead as the huge shape closed in on her. Something caught her around the waist, pulling her up as if she were made of paper. Her back slammed against something hard . . . muscular. The remembered feeling of skin on skin broke through her panic and she realized it was Flint, trying to "save" her. She went limp then, letting him drag her up to the surface and onto the floating raft.

"Are you OK? Arden?" He leaned over her, tense

with concern, as she lay flat on her back like a beached whale, sputtering water she'd swallowed because of him. "You OK?"

"Just what the hell did you think you were doing?" she lashed out at him when she caught her breath.

"I was . . . trying to . . . help you," he mumbled distractedly.

"Help me? I almost drowned because of you!"

The anguished look on his face made her realize how upset he was but struck her funny at the same time and she started laughing hysterically.

At first amazed, then immensely relieved, Flint broke up too. "Thank God, you're all right."

"Next time," she sniffed, salt water stinging her nose, "don't assume I'm so helpless."

"You're anything but helpless, dammit," he joked, smoothing the wet tangles of hair off her face. "I was hoping a little mouth-to-mouth resuscitation might be needed." A last strand of hair was caught in the corner of her mouth. Flint caressed it into place, his darkening gaze lingering on her wet, parted lips like a kiss. "I think I'll give you mouth-to-mouth anyway," he whispered thickly, "just in case." Before she could stop him he was kissing her, his wet, salty mouth pressing on hers with a hungry urgency that left her breathless, drawing her into a sensual undertow that threatened to overwhelm her.

How could one kiss have such an effect? Arden wondered, dragging her mouth away with great difficulty. "I can't . . . breathe."

"Good! That's what you do to me," his voice grated against her cheek, "you take my breath away . . . you shake me all up . . ." He buried his warm, wet face in the hollow of her shoulder. "God, when I saw you go under . . . and you didn't come up again . . ." He punctuated his words with desperate little kisses, working his way back up her long, delicate throat. "If anything had happened to you, I . . ." The rest was left unsaid but there was no mistaking the message written in his smoky eyes, spilling over into his cradling embrace, the bittersweet tenderness of his kiss when his mouth sought hers again.

The intensity of his feelings threw her completely at first, making it impossible for her to stop him, and Arden quickly found herself being drawn as inexorably as driftwood to the edge of a vortex. She meant to pull away before she was sucked down into it, past retrieving, but all she could do was moan as his mouth moved hungrily on hers. When his arms tightened around her in response, crushing her to him as though he never wanted to let go of her, she returned his embrace passionately.

As it had that night in the car, her body responded to him all by itself, instantly and completely. Her mouth opened under his, eager for the taste and feel of him, for the deep thrusts of his tongue which filled her up yet left her hungry for more. When he covered her with his body, all wet and slippery and smelling of the sea, she felt as though she were truly drowning now and grabbed onto him as if to keep from going under. His response set off a tidal wave of feeling that was almost scary in its intensity, sweeping away the few remaining doubts trying to surface in her mind. Instead of protesting when his powerful hands slid from around her back to swallow up her breasts while he lowered his head to cover them with avid little kisses, Arden dug her fingers convulsively into his hair, pulling him even closer as her body arched to meet his ravenous mouth.

Moaning deeply, Flint pressed his hips against her so she could feel the full extent of his desire. When he began to move sensuously against her, Arden found herself answering his rhythm as the raft swayed softly, hypnotically beneath them. In a daze, she watched his fingers hook onto the edge of her top and pull it down with one impatient motion, her breasts spilling into his waiting hands, taut nipples ready for his eager mouth.

"You're so beautiful," he whispered, his warm breath tickling one rosy tip before his mouth closed hungrily on it.

Arden cried out with pleasure she never knew existed. Wanting to kiss him, she lifted her head—and suddenly caught sight of a strange light flashing from the villa. It blinked down from the stone wall edging the deck like a double reflection of the sun bouncing off a mirror . . . or a pair of binoculars. Whatever it was, it startled her back to reality. Still oblivious to anything but his need for her, Flint released one swollen nipple only to try to capture the other.

"Stop!" Covering herself with one arm, Arden used the other to hold him off. His surprise made it easy for her to twist away from him and roll onto her stomach.

"What's . . . wrong?" he mumbled with some difficulty.

"Look!" Arden pointed towards the double flash of light she now knew had to be binoculars. Then she sat up quickly and struggled to cover herself. "Someone's watching us."

"What?" Turning around, Flint squinted up at the villa.

"Binoculars . . . someone's watching us," she repeated, tugging her top into place with boneless fingers as she fought to regain her usual composure while everything inside her was still shaking. She couldn't believe he had done this to her again, turned her into someone she couldn't recognize, making her lose all control.

"Looks like binoculars all right," he muttered tersely.

"Everything's a game with you people, isn't it?" she turned on him angrily.

"You don't think I had anything to do with that," he asked a bit breathlessly, obviously struggling to get himself back under control also, "do you?"

Arden glared at him silently. She didn't know what to think. She knew he couldn't have faked the depth of feeling he'd just revealed, but still . . .

"You can't believe that," he pleaded, running a warm hand soothingly down her back only to arouse her even more.

"Don't. She's still watching us. It's Gayle . . . I just know it is."

"So what? She has no claims on me. Besides, how much can she see from that distance? But if that's what she wants," he added in a voice thick with earlier emotions, "then let's really give her something to look at." He reached for her again but Arden scrambled to the other side of the raft.

"She was right. This is the real reason you asked me here!"

"What if it is?" He smiled wryly. "Is that so terrible?"

Expecting a denial, Arden didn't have an answer . . . or was it that somewhere deep inside she'd suspected as much from the start? She even found herself wondering whether that might have been the real reason she accepted the offer.

"I came here to write a book!" she insisted as if he were giving her an argument about it. "But since that was never your intention, I . . ."

"I never said that," he interrupted coolly. "That's what you said."

"Well, you haven't kept either one of my conditions so there's no point in my staying on here." She jumped to her feet and, although the raft swayed dangerously, she managed to keep her balance without taking the hand he stretched out to her. "I'm taking the first ferry back to the mainland tomorrow morning."

Flint started to say something but shrugged wordlessly instead, the strong, beautiful lines of his face hardening into a scornful mask. When Arden jumped off the raft, half-swimming, half-wading back to shore, he didn't come after her. She quickly gathered her things together and made her way back up the cobblestone path to the villa. She turned to look back only once—when she was far enough away so that he wouldn't see her. Flint was standing at the end of the jetty, outlined against the blazing sky for a moment before he disappeared into the lighthouse. The brilliant colors of the sunset transformed everything they touched, turning the sea, the beach, the entire island into an earthly paradise so achingly beautiful it made her want to cry.

8

Arden wished she hadn't packed so quickly because the rest of the evening stretched endlessly before her. She'd already taken the longest bath of her life and washed her hair twice. To avoid seeing Flint again, she hadn't gone down to dinner. She might as well have done so, since she couldn't stop thinking about him anyway and it would have helped pass the time. Besides, she was so hungry now that her stomach was growling at her.

With a sigh of self-disgust, she reread a paragraph in a national news magazine for the fourth time. Cursing under her breath, she tossed the magazine onto the armchair she'd just vacated and went striding irritably over to the picture window.

A perfectly round silver sphere, looking larger and brighter than the moon she was used to in New York, gleamed in the black velvet sky studded with more stars than she'd ever seen outside of a planetarium, illuminating the unreal beauty of the cove.

"Wouldn't you know there'd be a full moon?" Arden muttered bitterly, as if he'd ordered it especially, another one of his seductive ploys. "Well, that explains everything . . . a full moon is supposed to bring out the crazies." She couldn't help laughing at the craziness inherent in her talking out loud to herself—a habit she'd acquired since meeting the impossible Mr. Masters.

In spite of herself, Arden gazed longingly out at the lighthouse. There were no lights on inside, but its sharp outline was visible in the moonlight, as was the marina at the other end of the cove. She was even able to make out the rectangular shape of the raft. . . .

The rush of images that filled Arden's mind at the sight of the raft caught her unawares. She shut her eyes to block them out but instead shut out what was left of reality. Once again she tasted his warm, salty mouth, felt his eager hands swallowing up her breasts, the arousing hardness of his body on hers, all wet and slippery and smelling of the sea. . . .

With a determined effort she forced her eyes open, dragging herself away from the view and the disturbing memories it evoked. She wished she could blame the quivering in the pit of her stomach on simple hunger, but she was never one to lie to herself. Besides, on what would she blame her suddenly erratic heartbeat? The man had a devastating effect on her and there was no use denying it. It was a good thing she was leaving in the morning if just the thought of him was enough to seduce her . . . especially since she had never wanted to be seduced so desperately in her whole life.

There, she said it. She admitted it. It was true!

She couldn't understand why it had taken her so long to face it. The reason she'd gotten so angry with him on the raft, she just realized, wasn't that he'd all but admitted bringing her there under false pretenses, but that he'd forced her to acknowledge her real feelings about him. Now that she had, she couldn't possibly deny them, and the relationship they had had was no longer possible. But neither was the one he sought.

Flint was obviously infatuated with her, yet, just as obviously, all he wanted was an exciting but casual fling, something she'd always been incapable of. Yet for the first time in her life, she was seriously tempted. The two close encounters they'd had had given her a glimpse of the exciting and wonderful lover he would be. She felt sure that making love with him would be the most extraordinary experience she'd ever had . . . or would ever have. She knew that, just as she knew, with unshakable certainty, that if they ever did go to bed she would be hooked for good.

Arden stopped in the middle of the room and realized that she had literally been going around in circles. Shaking her head at herself, she went slowly, deliberately back to the armchair, seating herself with a composure she couldn't help being proud of, until she realized that she was sitting on the magazine. She tugged it out from under her and threw it clear across the room. It slammed up against one of the valises parked next to the door before landing, face down, on the carpet.

Anyway, it would never work out. In spite of the undeniably powerful attraction they felt for one another, they had nothing in common. Their personalities and life-styles were as diametrically opposed as what each of them wanted from a relationship. But just as she'd never presume to change Flint, she wasn't about to make herself over to suit him. She refused to be like Felicia or Gayle, the kind of woman he obviously preferred. And though, by his own admission, her lack of sexual sophistication was something new and intriguing to him, how long would it be before the novelty wore off and he went back to his original preference?

That surprisingly painful thought propelled Arden out of the armchair again. She stood there at a complete loss for a moment before continuing purposefully over to where the magazine lay all crumpled up. Retrieving it, she carefully smoothed out the pages before putting it down on the handcarved coffee table overflowing with the latest magazines. She then proceeded to make a neat little pile out of them.

The only sensible thing to do was to stop now while she was still capable of making a rational decision, before she got emotionally involved and lost all control. If only he didn't affect her the way he did, everything would be so simple. But all he had to do was touch her and somehow everything in her opened up to him, releasing a flood of feelings and longings that left her totally defenseless. She knew he didn't mean to affect her that way and would run like hell once he realized how she felt. That's why it was better for both of them if she left before her love for him grew to where . . .

Arden sank to her knees but still had to grab onto the coffee table to steady herself. "Oh, you fool, what have you done?" she wailed out loud. "You've fallen in love with him . . . how could you have been so dumb!"

Before she could recover from this startling self-revelation, there was a polite but determined knock on the door. It grew even more determined when, unable to move from the spot, Arden didn't answer it.

"Just . . . a minute," she yelled when she finally made her way over to the door. Flint wouldn't dare come here, she assured herself, not with his pride . . . or would he? She clutched the front of her battered old robe automatically, making sure it was closed properly. "Who is it?" she demanded defensively through the closed door as if she were still living in New York.

"It's Mrs. McNally."

"Oh, Mrs. McNally," Arden mumbled apologetically as she opened the door, feeling relieved and disappointed at the same time. "I'm sorry, I . . . I'm not dressed," she offered as an explanation for what she knew must seem rather peculiar behavior outside of a large city.

"I'm sorry to be disturbing you, Miss," the housekeeper said with her delightful touch of a brogue, though the tone of her voice was uncharacteristically chilly. "I just wanted to make sure you were all right."

"I'm fine . . . thank you."

"You didn't come down to dinner this evening," the older woman scolded, "so I brought you up a tray." A curt toss of her neatly coiffed head indicated the food cart resting parallel to the wall behind her.

"You shouldn't have gone to all that trouble, Mrs. McNally . . . but thanks very much."

"Don't be thanking *me,*" she grumbled, pushing the cart through the doorway. "It's Mr. Flint you should be thanking."

"Flint told you to bring my dinner up?" Arden asked with surprise while holding the door open for her.

"That's right," Mrs. McNally informed her belligerently, "and don't you go telling him I told you neither." She wheeled the cart past Arden, taking careful note of the suitcases. "You're still planning on leaving us, then?"

"Yes. Tomorrow morning."

"That's a damn fool thing to do, if you don't mind my saying so, Miss!"

"What?"

Mrs. McNally shook her head disapprovingly as she continued pushing the cart over to the dining alcove. "You'll be sorely missed, let me tell you that."

"Hardly, Mrs. McNally." Arden closed the door behind her with a sad smile. "But it's nice of you to say so."

"I wasn't speaking for myself," she snapped. "It's Mr. Flint I was talking about."

Arden was too surprised to answer. All she could do was stare dumbly as the housekeeper started lifting a heavy silver warming cover off a huge tray on the cart. "Here," she said, recovering, "let me help you with that."

Before Arden could get to her, Mrs. McNally was already sliding the cover, which was almost as big as she was, onto the bottom shelf of the cart. "I'm in no need of help," she stated proudly.

Arden didn't doubt it for a moment. Though the woman was half her size and more than twice her age, she was still quite formidable—especially when she was angry, as she clearly was now. Arden couldn't think what she had done to cause such a change in Mrs. McNally's usually friendly manner.

"And just when I was giving thanks to Saint Bridget that he finally found himself a decent girl," she muttered bitterly, banging a heated plate down on the table for good measure.

"I think you misunderstand the . . . situation," Arden protested, feeling a warm flush spread over her face. "I was hired by Mr. Masters to . . . "

"I'm not one to be misunderstanding things, Miss," Mrs. McNally interrupted imperiously, fixing Arden with a pair of emerald green eyes whose brightness and vitality were undiminished by time or the hardships of life. "No one needs to be telling me what's what. I'm not saying he's an easy man. No one knows that better than I. But you'll have to go some to find a finer one!" She punctuated that remark by slapping a serving platter down next to the plate, making Arden fear for the safety of the glass-topped table. "Roast pork with yellow rice and black beans," she announced curtly. "Go on and eat it before it gets cold."

"That looks delicious, Mrs. McNally," Arden exclaimed, grateful for the change of subject. Though the conversation had wrecked her appetite, she had to admit that everything looked scrumptious. "You really shouldn't have gone to all this trouble."

"It's himself I should be bringing a tray of food to," she agreed heatedly, "since he never once touched his dinner tonight . . . and him with his glorious appetite!" She glared at Arden, holding her completely responsible. "I've never seen the man in such a state!"

Arden felt that strange quivering in the pit of her stomach again, that same funny little skip between heartbeats.

"You're not looking so good yourself," Mrs. McNally allowed with a trace of apology in her voice. "Come . . . sit yourself down here. You must be half-starved. That dollop of cottage cheese you had for lunch was so small you couldn't have covered a postage stamp with it." She steered Arden into the chair with the no-nonsense concern of a mother hen. "Go on now . . . eat your dinner."

Caught in a rush of conflicting emotions, Arden picked up her fork like an obedient five-year-old, but she was too preoccupied even to think of food. Why hadn't Flint eaten his dinner? Was he upset because she was leaving? Or was it merely hurt pride? Either way, he'd had the consideration to arrange for her dinner. Every time she figured she had him pegged, he pulled another switch on her. He certainly was the most complex, unpredictable man she'd ever met. The realization that she would never see him again suddenly hit her, harder than she would ever have believed possible.

"Are you all right, Miss Arden?" she heard Mrs. McNally inquiring in the warm, friendly tone she remembered.

Arden nodded reassuringly, looking down into her plate so the housekeeper wouldn't see the tears filling her eyes, and started pushing her food around with her fork.

"Another one who's gone and lost their appetite," the older woman remarked pointedly, "and for the same reason I'm thinking." She poured a glass of imported white wine and set it down in front of Arden. "Here, this'll do you a bit of good."

Arden downed several gulps before she was able to regain her composure.

"It's not like me to go sticking my nose in other people's business," Mrs. McNally insisted softly, "but are you sure you're doing the right thing?"

"Yes." Arden looked back up into the housekeeper's concerned face with a sad but grateful smile. "It's better this way . . . for both of us."

"Well, I suppose you know what you're doing." She sighed heavily. "I know *you're* not a feather-brain like some others. Good luck to you then." She squeezed Arden's hand in a warm, impulsive gesture before reaching quickly for the wine bottle and refilling Arden's glass with her typical efficiency.

"Enjoy your dinner, Miss. When you're finished, just leave the cart outside. Rosa will come and take it away."

"Thank you, Mrs. McNally," Arden said sincerely, "for . . . everything."

"Not at all," she replied politely before bustling over to the door, pausing only to heave another great sigh at the sight of the packed suitcases. "But I don't mind telling you, Miss, you're a damn fool if you let a man like Flint Masters get away," she couldn't resist tossing over her shoulder before she slammed the door behind her, "a damn fool!"

"You're damn right, Mrs. McNally." Arden laughed out loud at herself. "And you don't even know how big a fool I am . . . even I never knew that till now!"

She was suddenly feeling as elated as she'd been depressed just minutes before. Her appetite had returned with a vengeance and she set about attacking her food, though she barely tasted it after the second or third morsel. Her feverish mind was too busy picking the bones of her conversation with Mrs. McNally.

Had Flint "lost his glorious appetite for the same reason" . . . would she be "sorely missed" . . . and was he really "in such a state" because she was leaving? Could it be possible that he had some feeling for her after all? That he didn't consider her just an offbeat addition to his collection of playmates as she'd feared? If she thought there was even a chance that he cared for her, she'd never be able to leave him. . . .

And then she'd look like a damn fool in front of everybody.

The usually dominant sensible side of Arden carefully crossed her knife and fork on the half-full plate and folded her napkin neatly beside it. She was willing to admit that Mrs. McNally was a sincere, well-meaning person, but her version of the facts might have been colored by her practically maternal attachment to Flint. The state he was in at dinner could just as easily be attributed to the anger and hurt pride of a man accustomed to women falling into his irresistible arms, and bed, with little or no effort on his part. If she wasn't just another notch on his gun and he really cared about her, then why hadn't he made some attempt to stop her from leaving? Flint Masters didn't strike her as a man who would allow anything or anybody he wanted to get away from him, at least not without a fight. Yet he hadn't made a single attempt to contact her. Not even a phone call!

By the time Arden was ready for bed and he still hadn't called, though it was well past midnight, even her newly emergent "damn fool" side had to admit that Mrs. McNally's interpretation of Flint's behavior had been wishful thinking. The fact that she was now convinced she'd made the right decision was precious little comfort to her as she tossed and turned, unable to fall asleep.

The irritatingly bright moonlight streaming through the transparent drapes wasn't helping any. Nor was the view of the lighthouse all lit up like a Christmas tree inside. Arden's conviction that Flint was in there, finishing off with Gayle what he had started with her on the raft, didn't make for sweet dreams either.

The shrill, insistent sound penetrated Arden's dream, became part of it, and finally shattered it, dragging her reluctantly back to consciousness. It took her a moment to realize where she was and what was happening. She couldn't believe it was already time for her wake-up call. She was sure she hadn't slept for more than a couple of hours.

Turning over in bed with a groggy sigh, she reached blindly for the telephone. "OK . . . thank you," she murmured into it, still half-asleep.

"I'm sorry, I didn't mean to wake you up," answered a voice disgustingly wide awake for that time of the morning. He didn't sound all that sorry either.

Arden's eyes flew open. "I'm awake," she insisted though she couldn't remember ever waking up that fast before. "I was just getting myself together . . . to make the ferry."

"Take your time," Flint drawled sarcastically, "the 7:30 ferry left two hours ago."

"What? But I left a wake-up call."

"Then you should have answered it."

"But I never heard it," she muttered wonderingly to herself. It wasn't like her to oversleep when she had an appointment. The wake-up call had just been an added precaution.

"You know what Freud says about that," he commented wryly. "Subconsciously you never wanted to catch that ferry."

"What?" Is that why he was finally calling her, to discuss Sigmund Freud's theory of the subconscious? "But what would Freud have said if he had known that wasn't the last ferry?" she countered defensively. "I can still make the one at six this evening."

"I think he'd have said you're not going to make that one either because . . ."

"Well, too bad he's not around to see me off!"

"Because," Flint insisted, ignoring her interruption, "I'm sure he'd agree that you're too mature a lady to scrap an entire project just because we had a . . . slight misunderstanding."

"A slight misunderstanding?" she repeated incredulously. Is that all it had meant to him?

"And he'd have been surprised, as I am, to find you acting so unprofessionally."

"Me unprofessional?" Arden started to explode before catching herself. She refused to let him do that to her again. That's how he'd talked her into coming here in the first place, by appealing to her professional ethics. Well, two could play that game. "Let me remind you that *you* were the one who broke our agreement, not me."

"You're right," he admitted, leaving her speechless. By agreeing with her he'd effectively demolished all the arguments she had been preparing. "I've been doing some self-analysis as well," he continued without missing a beat, making her wonder whether this little speech had been carefully rehearsed, "and I have to admit I've been remiss. I've been so involved with closing this new deal that I haven't been able to give our project the attention it deserves. But now that the deal is almost finalized, I'll soon be able to devote all my time to you."

At first, Arden wasn't sure what he meant by that but decided—shades of Freud again—that she was projecting her own feelings onto him, because his tone couldn't have been more impersonal.

"I'm afraid it's no use," she said firmly.

"Why not?"

"Because I know now that we're just too . . . different and we could never . . . work together."

"You're wrong. We'd be great together." He laughed unexpectedly, a deep, sexy laugh that made her nerve endings tingle.

"It's just not going to work out!"

"But it will . . . if you give it a chance," he pleaded. "Just give it a chance, that's all I ask!"

Once again, Arden sensed a double meaning to his words. There was no denying the very real emotion in his plea but it must have slipped out in spite of him because he was quick to cover it up.

"I've already instructed Mrs. McNally to let you into the lighthouse as you requested," he resumed in his business voice. "My study's on the second floor. I think you'll find what you're looking for in the binders I've left for you on top of my desk. They contain the more important excerpts from diaries I've kept over the years and some . . . recent notations." He paused to draw in a long, ragged breath. "I suggest that you take a bottle of extra-strength aspirin along with you," he added in an attempt at a joke.

Arden suddenly realized how difficult this was for him. She knew how fanatical he was about his privacy but felt, instinctively, that there was more to it than that. Was he about to expose some deep, dark secret from his past as she'd once half-jokingly wondered? And, if so, why was he doing it?

"That's what you want, isn't it?" he prompted sarcastically, shattering her thoughts. "To discover the *real* Flint Masters?"

"Yes!" Arden admitted excitedly. There was no use denying it. Flint couldn't know why it meant so much to her, but he obviously knew it did or he wouldn't be using it to get what he wanted . . . if only she knew what that was.

"Well, you're about to find out finally, aren't you?" he muttered caustically.

Once again, Arden was at a loss to understand the strange bitterness that tinged his voice whenever they talked about the book. "That *is* why I came here . . . why *you* asked me here." She reacted defensively, determined to hide the hurt his bitterness caused her. "How can I write a book about you unless I find out about the *real* you?"

"You may find more than you bargained for!"

"What?"

"Then I'll inform Mrs. McNally that . . ."

"What did you mean by that?" Arden interrupted angrily, unable to go on playing whatever game it was he was playing this time.

"Just that the . . . job might be more than you care to handle . . . once you fully realize what you're getting yourself into."

He sighed heavily. "However, if you decide that it is, you can still make the six o'clock ferry. I won't be back till after seven so . . ."

"I don't understand any of this," Arden interrupted impatiently. "I thought you wanted me to stay . . . and now you're telling me it's all right to leave!"

"It's not what . . . I want that counts." His voice was practically inaudible. Arden had to press her ear closer to the receiver to hear him at all. "You've got to want it too."

"Want what? What are we talking about?" she implored. "I've had the feeling, all along, that we're not really talking about what we're talking about!"

"I thought I made myself pretty clear," Flint said carefully, after an interminable pause.

It was that need for a pause, that too-careful tone of voice that made Arden feel she was right and finally blurt out what she could no longer hold back. "And *I* think what we're really talking about is what happened between us yesterday . . . on the raft."

"You don't have to worry about that, I told you," he insisted, having totally misunderstood her. "I intend to keep our agreement from now on. That won't happen again. Unless *you* want it to." He waited for her reaction. An audible gasp was all she was capable of. "Next time, and I think there will be a next time, you'll have to come to me."

With the dial tone whining in her ear, Arden became convinced that not even Freud could have unraveled the complexities of Flint Masters's mind. But, as she hung up, a rush of excitement filled her at the thought of being so near to finding the missing pieces of the puzzle—an excitement strangely tinged with fear.

9

I hope you don't mind my saying how pleased I am that you'll be staying on after all, Miss." The tiny housekeeper beamed up at Arden as they made their way down the jetty to the lighthouse.

"Thank you, Mrs. McNally." Arden smiled back gratefully. "Especially since you had something to do with it."

"Ah, it wasn't my doing at all." Bright green eyes crinkled up, twinkling with humor. "It's all them candles I've been lighting to Saint Bridget all these years."

Arden laughed. "Then you must thank her for me the next time you speak to her."

"I already have, Miss," Mrs. McNally stated simply. "If you only knew how Mr. Flint helped me when poor Mr. McNally, God rest his soul, took sick. Bad sick he was . . . and for years. And me all alone in this country with no job and no hopes of finding one. . . ." She paused as memory became painful reality for a moment, turning her face away to hide the tears stinging her eyes.

Sensing the strong pride in the woman, Arden stifled an impulse to reach out to her. Mrs. McNally dug deep into her apron pocket and came up with a large metal ring with a landlord's assortment of keys dangling from it. Concentrating on the task of finding the proper key seemed to help her regain control of herself.

"Then you'd understand why I feel about Mr. Flint the way I do," she continued in her usual feisty tone. "And I'm not the only one, mind you. Ask anyone here who works for him." She came to a sudden halt, a few feet from the lighthouse. "They're the ones you should be talking to if you want to know about Flint Masters. Every one of them has a story to tell . . . but you won't find *that* printed in the papers," she added bitterly, resuming the walk. "Ah, yes, it's about time that man found some real happiness." She slanted a warm, embarrassingly grateful smile at Arden.

"Mrs. McNally, I wish I could say that what you're . . . thinking about Flint and me is true," Arden said ruefully, "but it's not."

"What are you saying, girl?" The older woman

laughed. "Haven't I seen it with my own two eyes the way either of you looks when the other so much as walks into the room? The way you two feel about each other is as plain as the nose on your face."

"But we don't feel the *same* way," Arden blurted out painfully. "Don't you understand?"

"No, I surely don't." Mrs. McNally stopped in front of the cast-iron door of the lighthouse, the key she was about to insert poised in midair while she waited for an explanation—as though she wasn't about to budge until she got one.

"I know that Flint is . . . attracted to me," Arden admitted with difficulty, "but that's how he feels about other women too."

"Does he now?" Mrs. McNally snapped defensively as if Arden were attacking the integrity of her very own son. "So how is it then that you're the first woman he's ever allowed into the lighthouse?"

"What?"

"That's so. Except for myself and Rosa who comes to clean. He's never let any of those . . . other women so much as set foot in here!" She shoved the key into the lock, turning it forcefully.

"But that's just because of the research I'm doing," Arden explained once she'd recovered from her initial surprise.

"Is that the excuse he's using then?" the feisty housekeeper muttered. "And you believed him?"

Arden didn't know whom to believe anymore: Flint, Gayle, Mrs. McNally, or herself. The whole situation reminded her of *Rashomon*: four different versions of the same story, each one colored by the perceptions and prejudices of the storyteller.

The heavy door swung open under Mrs. McNally's determined push. "Well, I suppose you're going to have to find out for yourself, Miss." She stepped aside to let Arden into the lighthouse.

As Arden closed the cast-iron door behind her, she thought she knew how Alice must have felt when she went through the looking glass. Though remodeled, the lighthouse still belonged to a world and time that were light-years away from the villa. Its circular stone walls were covered with medieval tapestries and old Spanish muskets and swords, and its ceilings were fifteen feet high. It reminded Arden of the illustrations in a book of fairy tales. She could easily imagine Rapunzel leaning out of one of those stained-glass windows towards her lover, her hair a golden ladder. The wind sighed all through the lighthouse, playing an eerie duet with the rhythmic, almost hypnotic sound of the sea dashing itself to bits against the rocky foundations. In a kind of daze, Arden roamed from floor to floor, searching out clues, making detailed notes about everything she observed.

A large, old-fashioned kitchen dominated the first floor. The rough-hewn oak table at its center was larger than her entire kitchenette back in New York. It matched the cabinets which ringed the wall, cleverly disguising all the most up-to-date appliances. A smoke-blackened kettle hung from a chain in the middle of the enormous fireplace once used for cooking. The thick iron spit crossing it was long enough to hold a full-grown steer. Gleaming copper pans in all sizes and shapes hung suspended from pegs in the wall alongside antique cooking utensils. The kitchen was a gourmet cook's dream but it had the strangely forlorn feeling of abandoned or rarely lived-in houses.

Flint's bedroom on the top floor was the most unusual room in the lighthouse. It was, without doubt, the most unique room Arden had ever seen. It must have been the observation deck once because the wall was a circle of glass, ringed outside by a metal walkway reminiscent of a crow's nest on a galleon. A pair of seagulls were currently using it as a perch. The completely transparent wall created the illusion of being suspended in midair in the seamless blue of sky and sea which stretched clear to the horizon. Except for the circular bed in the center of the room, there was no other furniture. On closer inspection, Arden found that the custom-made platform it rested on like a foam rubber cloud concealed drawers, ample storage space, even a built-in stereo system.

But the room that most fascinated her was the combination living room and study on the center floor. It was the room in which Flint obviously spent the most time and into which he had put most of himself.

The circular room had been divided into back-to-back semicircles. The living room area was pretty much what she'd expected, given what she already knew about Flint. It was so—*sensuous* was the only word she could think of to describe it—that Arden questioned Mrs. McNally's claim that Flint had never brought any of his women there.

A modular sofa, made up entirely of cream-colored velvet pillows, formed one of the semicircles. It faced a fireplace displaying various coats of arms and was flanked by a bar and a complete stereo rack system. Flint had an impressive collection of records and tapes ranging from jazz to classical. The floor was carpeted in wall-to-wall flokati. The fluffy white sheep's wool was so thick that she couldn't understand the need for the velvet throw pillows scattered about. Kicking off her sandals impulsively, Arden dug her bare toes into the long, curly fleece. It was such a delicious sensation that she couldn't help wondering what it would feel like to lie there next to Flint, listening to music, letting her whole body sink into it while . . .

Dragging herself away from the living room and the disturbing thoughts it evoked, Arden continued over to the semicircle of bookcases that partitioned off the study area. They were filled with rare, leather-bound books and priceless first editions. Only someone who loved books as much as she did could have spent the time and money needed to amass such a collection. She would never have expected that of him.

The rest of the furnishings had to have been as carefully and lovingly collected. The intricately carved Renaissance table he used as a desk, as well as the hand-tooled leather chairs and beautifully displayed works of art, might have belonged to a Florentine merchant prince rather than a twentieth-century business tycoon. The intensely masculine tone of the study was softened by an exquisite medieval tapestry that time had faded into the most delicate pastels and warmed by the deep rich tones of a luxurious Persian rug.

For the first time, Arden felt that she'd caught a glimpse of the real man behind the myth, and what she saw thrilled and frightened her at the same time: she could lose herself irretrievably in this world, in such a man.

She believed Mrs. McNally's statement now; she even thought she understood why he'd never allowed anyone else in here. This world he'd created for himself was his only refuge from the outside world, the only place where he could really be himself. She wondered whether it bothered him that he had no one to share it with. Since Arden felt that Flint could have practically any woman he wanted, she decided that he must prefer it this way, though she couldn't understand why. There were still so many unanswered questions about him. Hoping finally to find the answers, Arden curled up on the flokati carpet in front of the fireplace with the diaries he'd left for her as he had promised. She hesitated as she was about to open the first binder and suddenly recalled his words of warning: "You may find more than you bargained for." When she opened it, her hands were trembling and she was literally holding her breath.

It wasn't the usual diary, kept on a daily basis and detailing everyday happenings. It was a collection of loose-leaf pages written at various times in his life and spilling over with the most intense emotions. It was as if he'd had no one to talk to about these special events and feelings so he'd poured them out on paper. The earliest ones were written when he was barely ten years old and cried out his pain and anger at his mother's desertion. The sense of loss contained in those pages was so palpable that it hurt Arden to read them, especially since she knew from her own childhood what loss and loneliness were.

Flint never wrote about his mother again, nor was Arden able to find any pictures of her when she went through the photo album later on. Her face and figure had been cut out of every family photo, leaving a gaping hole. Arden found it difficult to believe that the tall, frail man with the shabby clothes and dreamer's face could be Flint's father. They were so totally different from one another. The beautiful boy with the curly black hair and startling eyes seemed to be more mature, surer of himself than the man—as if he had to be strong for both of them. Arden never found out the reason Flint's mother walked out on them but she was pretty sure it was the dire poverty exposed in those faded snapshots.

Reading between the lines of the next batch of entries, written a few years later, confirmed her feeling. They were so without emotion as to be suspect. All the teenager in these pages longed for was money and success. There was something desperate about his single-minded determination to achieve them—as if they were the answer to everything. It would be years before he proudly documented his first business success.

After a lull of several more years, there was another spurt of writing, but this was as ecstatic as only a young man in love for the first time could be.

Her name was Holly and, according to the joyous entry announcing their engagement, she was as accomplished as she was beautiful. The next few pages detailed plans for the villa Flint was building for her as a wedding present. Then, after a short lull and without explanation, came three legal-size pages filled on both sides, almost impossible to read because the handwriting was distorted by drunkenness and intense emotion.

Arden pored over them for over an hour before she was able to piece the story together: the beautiful and accomplished Holly had broken off their engagement in order to marry another man, one richer and more powerful than Flint had been at the time. According to the date, that was almost ten years ago but the pain and rage filling those pages were as shatteringly alive as if he'd written them yesterday.

Arden was so shaken that she had to stop reading. She'd always sensed a capacity for deep emotion behind that sardonic mask of his but she'd never expected anything like this. Or that someone else's pain could hurt her so much. She understood why he'd always been so secretive about his past now. And his bitter postscript—"Can't win with them . . . poor . . . rich . . . they're still going to leave you"— finally explained his defensive, sometimes downright contemptuous attitude towards women. What Arden still couldn't understand was why Flint would expose such painful memories to her. Finding the answers had also uncovered more questions.

With a bewildered sigh, she removed her reading glasses to rub the ache beginning to throb between her eyes. She felt chilled all of a sudden, too, and wondered whether it was a reaction to what she'd just read—no, not read, experienced. Whatever it was, her halter top and denim skirt had been designed to keep her cool, not warm. She rubbed her bare arms and legs vigorously while she seriously considered lighting a fire. Normally, she wouldn't have dared to do so in someone else's home, but the logs had already been piled on top of one another with pieces of newspaper stuffed between the cracks, and a tall brass match holder had been placed within arm's reach. Arden was sure that Flint, anticipating her wish, had set it all up for her. She went ahead and started a fire. It gave her a chance to concentrate on something else, to get away from the confusing thoughts and feelings threatening to overwhelm her.

As Arden basked in the welcome warmth of the fire, she wondered what time it was. Sunlight was still streaming through the stained-glass windows but from a lower point in the sky. The multicolored pattern it cast over the flokati carpet was deeper in color than before; it was obviously later than she thought.

She felt that she shouldn't be there when Flint returned. She didn't know what his reaction would be, or her own for that matter, and she'd had enough surprises for one day. But there were still a couple of pages left, so Arden decided to skim through them before leaving, even though she knew she could never write that book about him now. She felt a kind of fierce protectiveness towards him, a longing to shield him from any more pain. How could she expose the painful secrets of his past to people who were only interested in reading the latest bit of sensationalism? If she still felt compelled to read the last few pages, it was only because she longed to know him as deeply as possible—but as a woman, no longer as a writer. Slipping her glasses back on, Arden couldn't help wondering if it hadn't been that way from the start.

The last couple of pages must have been fairly recent entries because they weren't yellow with age around the edges like the others. Checking the date, she was amazed to find that they'd been written yesterday, obviously last night . . . and they were all about her!

They started out like a letter to himself, arguing the pros and cons of his feelings for her, but as they continued—the writing increasingly slurred by drink, key words misspelled, thoughts cut off in mid-sentence by doubts and despair—they became a confession of love and desire for her of such naked intensity that Arden was stunned.

"You may find more than you bargained for." Flint's cryptic remark finally made sense. Now she understood why he'd exposed his most intimate memories to her. It was his way of letting her know what he never could tell her. By letting her into the parts of his life he'd never shared with anyone else, he was proving to her how very special she was to him. Knowing how fanatical he was about his privacy, Arden fully realized what it must have cost him and it moved her deeply.

She was rereading the confession through a mist of ecstatic tears when she sensed that she wasn't alone, that someone was watching her intently. Looking up, she saw Flint standing just outside the semicircle created by the modular sofa. Everything in her quickened at the sight of him, making it impossible for her to say or do anything.

The battle he'd fought with himself in the letter was evident on his face. There were circles under his eyes, and lines of exhaustion etched the corners of his mouth, adding to his ravaged look. His hair was as rumpled as the expensive sports jacket he'd slung over one arm. Not moving, he quickly scanned the binders lying next to her on the carpet, tensing visibly when he recognized the pages she was still clutching in her hand. When he looked back up at her, his silvery eyes pleaded for her answer as if his very life depended on it.

There was so much Arden longed to tell him but it was all blind emotion, went too deep for words, and words were all she knew. She watched helplessly as the look in his eyes hardened, and his rugged features set into a mask.

"Working overtime?" he drawled sarcastically. "I keep forgetting how dedicated you are . . . to your work."

Arden struggled through the maze of unfamiliar emotions to find the words to explain but he cut her off before she got the chance.

"Well, I'm sure you found what you came for . . . more than even you could have hoped for," he added bitterly, tossing the jacket over the top of the sofa. "It should make for a very amusing book!"

The pages slid out of Arden's hand, fluttering

down to the carpet. Dropping her glasses on top of them, she rose slowly to her feet.

"I assume that's the reason you're still here. Isn't it?"

She started to protest again but realized it wouldn't do any good. There was only one answer really, and only one way to tell him. She went over to him and wrapped her arms around him, wordlessly.

With a strangled cry, Flint grabbed her, burying his tortured face in the hollow of her shoulder, in a tangle of golden hair. An overwhelming rush of love and tenderness filled her. Everything she'd felt when she read about his mother's desertion, his fiancée's betrayal, and his anguished confession of love for her was in it. She longed to give him all the love he'd lost, that he'd given up on yet wanted so desperately. Nothing else mattered to her anymore, not even what happened to her afterwards. All she cared about was the man she held cradled in her arms.

"I wasn't sure I'd find you here," he croaked against her shoulder, his breath a warm, jagged sigh on her bare skin.

"I'm here," she murmured reassuringly, pressing her whole body closer so he could feel for himself. "Right . . . here." Twining her fingers in his thick, silky hair, she drew his face up to hers. His silvery eyes fluttered open in amazement. She closed them again with a barrage of tender little kisses which she continued feathering all over his face until her lips found and caught his, muffling the groan deep in his throat.

As if that were all he'd been waiting for, he

tightened his arms around her, crushing her to him. "Yes . . . love me," he moaned on her mouth, "love me!"

The naked urgency of his plea touched something deep inside her, leaving her totally defenseless. There was no way she could deny him. Her mouth opened under his, welcoming the fierce thrust of his tongue as she gave herself up to him completely. The passion which had been smoldering beneath the surface ignited on contact. Everything seemed to explode in and around her at the same time. She felt his whole body go rigid with pleasure as hers melted utterly into his. His mouth was devouring her, unleashing a hunger in her that was just as overwhelming as his.

Gasping for breath, Arden dragged her mouth away from his but clung to him tightly.

"Are you all right?" Flint gasped, as out of breath as she was and looking just as dazed. "I didn't . . . hurt you?"

"No, I . . . it's . . ." She couldn't put a complete sentence together and wondered vaguely where all the clever words had gone.

"Yes . . . it is," he muttered thickly, having obviously understood her without words. "It's . . . unbelievable, I know." His hand moved softly from around her back to brush a strand of hair from her face. "After that first time, I kept telling myself I must have imagined it . . . that no one could be as sweet and warm as you are." Tucking the loose curl tenderly behind one ear, he moved to cup her chin. "But you're even more beautiful than I remembered." He drew her face back to his until their lips were so close they shared the same breath again. "I want you so much . . . so much."

The tip of his tongue glided sensually over her swollen lips, slowly tracing their outline before darting past them to torment the even-more-sensitive inner part. With a sharp little cry, Arden's tongue caressed his, craving it deep inside her. This time she was the passionate aggressor as her mouth told him of her love and desire without words. And he was the one who had to drag his mouth away.

"What are we doing . . . I mean, standing here like this?" He laughed breathlessly. "I don't know about you . . . but my legs feel like jelly." Releasing her, Flint staggered back a few steps to plop down on the top of the sofa, his long legs spread out in front of him. "Come here." Reaching out, he caught her around the waist, pulling her over to him. "Feel for yourself."

His thighs felt like anything but jelly to Arden as he tightened them around her hips, holding her against him in a vise of taut muscles, but they *were* shaking. Almost as much as she was. She had to rest both hands on his powerful shoulders to steady herself, but what she saw reflected in the smoky depths of his eyes left her even more shaken.

"I had to stop that," he murmured intensely, "or I would have thrown you down on that carpet and ravished you on the spot . . . and that's not how I want it to be with you." His strong hands slid gently up from her waist and over her bare back to tangle in the golden strands of her hair as they sought the halter's fastening. "I've wanted this so much, I can't tell you . . . too much to rush it." Finding the single closing, he unhooked it slowly.

Arden shivered involuntarily as the cool fabric slid smoothly down her heated skin, off her bare breasts to fall in a tiny, lilac heap on his lap. With a sharp intake of breath, he parted his lips as his smoky gaze swept over her hungrily, but his fingers continued to move slowly, seductively down her throat and shoulders, down past the slope of her breasts to linger erotically around their high, soft curves. Arden felt herself melting under the drugging warmth of his hands, the burning hunger in his eyes, as a curious molten thrill started spreading through her.

Flint's eyes never left her face, watching the play of emotions on it with a kind of wonder as his hands dropped to the tie belt holding her denim wraparound skirt closed. One tug and the bow came undone but he unwrapped her gently, like a precious, eagerly awaited gift.

"You're so lovely," he marveled when she finally stood before him naked. He took such unashamed pleasure in her body glowing softly in the firelight that Arden was amazed to find she felt no shame or embarrassment. "Your skin is like satin." He started to reach for her but stopped himself, standing up abruptly. "I want to feel you all over me," he explained thickly, moving to unbutton his shirt impatiently.

"No . . . let me!" It came tearing out of her, surprising her even more than him. But she couldn't deny her feelings for him even if she had wanted to. She ached for the sight and feel of him. She wanted to arouse him just as exquisitely as he aroused her . . . even though she wasn't quite sure how to go about it. Neil had made love to her a few times, but always in the dark as if they were doing something shameful, to be gotten over with as quickly as possible. She'd never dreamed it could be so natural, so piercingly beautiful.

Arden's hands seemed to know instinctively what to do even if she didn't, or maybe they'd learned their lesson from Flint's. They unbuttoned his shirt eagerly, trembling more from excitement than insecurity. Insinuating themselves inside the open shirt, they slowly caressed it off his shoulders, down his arms and back until it was lying in a heap with her clothes on the floor. Moving searchingly, erotically all over his powerful chest, they burrowed into the surprisingly soft, dark curls before following them down to his lean waist. They had no trouble opening the belt or the zipper on his pants but fumbled with the button inside the waistband that she didn't know would be there.

"I'm not very good at this," she explained even though she felt sure, as experienced as he was, he already knew that.

"You're doing . . . just fine," he murmured, a strange catch in his voice. He seemed oddly moved by what she was doing, which tugged at something inside her. When she went down on her knees before him, in order to ease his pants off, he wound his fingers tenderly in her hair. With growing urgency, Arden finished undressing him, eager to remove the last barrier between them, to have him finally revealed to her. . . .

All the pieces of the puzzle suddenly clicked into place. *This* was what she'd really been looking for, hoping to find—the intense passion and longing for love that she'd always sensed were buried deep inside him.

Following every curve and hollow of his body, she worked her way back up to his face, reading him with her fingers, memorizing the taste and feel of him with her mouth and hands.

"You're driving me up the wall," he groaned as her lips and hands continued tracing sensuous patterns on his skin.

"Are you cold?" she wondered out loud. "You're goose bumps all over."

"Here, feel how cold I am!" he ground out passionately. Clutching the rounded flesh of her bottom with burning hands, he pulled her hard up against the taut length of his body, pressing her hips into his so she could feel the full extent of his heat. Arden shivered uncontrollably. "Cold?" He laughed huskily, and found the answer with his mouth when he kissed her until they were both shaking. "I can't take much more of this."

Locking both arms under her bottom in a fierce hug, Flint lifted her several inches off the floor, taking the full weight and length of her body on his. "I've got to have you . . . all of you . . . right now!"

"Oh, yes," Arden moaned, burying her face in the hollow of his shoulder, her moist lips on the pulse beating violently in his throat. "Yes . . . please." She closed her eyes, giving herself up to the intoxicating smell and feel of his skin, to the strong, cradling motion of his body as he carried her upstairs to the bedroom. Winding her arms around his neck, she clung to him tightly as the whole world went spinning around her, round and round like the spiral staircase. Everything righted itself for a moment and then she was falling, still held in his strong embrace but falling backwards through space to crash-land softly onto the huge circular bed.

The feeling of his hard, vibrant body on hers was all that was left of reality. Even with her eyes open, Arden still felt as though she were floating in space. The glass hall which encircled them was invisible at night, enhancing the illusion that the room was suspended like the brilliant stars in a black velvet sky stretching out to infinity. The full moon seemed so close she felt she could reach up and touch it. It lit up the bedroom with a pale, translucent glow that shimmered all over her skin, turning her long, golden hair into a halo. And it was reflected in the depths of his silvery eyes when they swept over her longingly.

"God, I want you so much . . . but I don't want it to end either," he rasped wonderingly. "I never knew I could be so . . . greedy." Strong, demanding hands slid from around her back to swallow up the fullness of one breast and lift it slowly to his parted lips. His tongue curled around the rosy tip, exciting it to an aching tautness before his mouth closed over it.

Arden gasped as her body arched into him convulsively. Her hands sought to twine themselves in his hair but he slipped through her fingers to move down her body and cover it with feverish kisses and stinging, little love bites, sending soft, sharp waves of unbelievable pleasure rippling all through her.

"Please . . ." she implored, her slender arms

reaching out to pull him back up to her and put an end to the delicious torment, "please . . ."

"Yes," he breathed on her skin, "oh, yes . . ." Instead, his warm, wet mouth continued down to where her tan ended, to trace the outline of her swimsuit with his tongue. Parting her thighs, only to wrap them around him, he opened her up with soft burning kisses. Again and again he brought her to the brink only to stop as if he couldn't get enough of her, never wanted it to end. When he finally entered her, it was with a cry, a shudder that went right through her.

Arden felt herself unravelling, starting to come apart, and it frightened her, stalling the urgent rhythm of their movements. Flint was immediately aware of her confused attempt to hold back. He seemed to know it was because this was the first time this had ever happened to her.

"It's all right . . . just let go," he coaxed her tenderly while his body continued to urge her on with deep, powerful thrusts. "Don't be afraid . . . I've got you." Strong, sure arms tightened around her but instead of holding her together they snapped the last shred of resistance in her.

Her mind melted out even as her body seemed to fuse with his until she didn't know where she ended and he began. The world dissolved around her, rushing away from her at the speed of light, and she shattered into a million brilliant pieces, whirling out into space like the burnt-out shreds of an exploding star.

10

It had to be the most gloriously beautiful day since creation. At least that's how it looked to Arden when she floated out of the lighthouse door the next morning. The sun was blazing in a cloudless, azure sky and the air smelled good enough to bottle. The transparent sea was flowing fragments of pale green, turquoise, and cobalt blue. It lapped the rocks around the jetty with a languid, caressing motion, making a sound like drawn-out sighs.

She couldn't remember ever feeling so vibrantly alive, so intensely a part of everything around her.

She fully realized that her feelings were those of an eighteen-year-old in love for the first time, but for once she didn't question them. She had the rest of her life to be sensible. Today she was going to be ecstatically, childishly, absurdly happy.

She was tempted to spend the day on the beach but decided to remain in her room where Flint wouldn't have any trouble reaching her. It wasn't like Arden to wait by the telephone all day for a man's call, or to suffer such an awful letdown when she still hadn't heard from him by late afternoon.

She tried telling herself that Flint was a very busy man who was closing out an important deal today before flying to the mainland to pick up the usual weekend guests. But when she remembered that there was a phone in his car, as well as on the seaplane, she wondered whether she hadn't misunderstood him again. Hadn't last night been as extraordinary for him as it had been for her?

Curled up on the window seat, staring wistfully out at the lighthouse reflecting the deepening colors of the sky, Arden analyzed the events of the night before, trying to be as objective as possible.

They'd fallen asleep in a warm, moist tangle of arms and legs after making love and woke up a couple of hours later, refreshed but famished. Since neither of them could bear to break the spell they were still caught up in by going back to the villa, Flint ransacked the refrigerator in the kitchen where Mrs. McNally always kept food for him to snack on.

Wearing only a linen napkin draped over one arm, Flint set a large tray down in the center of the bed. It held an assortment of imported cheeses, smoked ham, potato chips, a tin of beluga caviar and one of anchovies, and a chilled bottle of champagne with two paper cups. Unashamedly naked, they sat Indian-fashion around the tray and proceeded to have a picnic in bed.

Arden had never felt so recklessly happy, nor had she ever seen Flint so open or relaxed. His face was still flushed from making love and was amazingly soft. There was none of the usual defensiveness in his manner, and he wore a slightly punchy grin even while he was eating. He was so piercingly beautiful to her that she had trouble swallowing at times. And the strange, new image of herself that she saw reflected in the loving wonder of his eyes was just as amazing to her.

Carrying on like a couple of love-struck kids, they polished off every last bit of food, in between kisses, topping it all off with champagne. For dessert, they had each other again.

Arden wasn't sure how long she slept that time but she was awakened by the sunrise lighting up the sky, spilling pastel reflections all over the covers. Flint was no longer in bed with her. She went looking for him and found him downstairs in the living room. He was sitting rather stiffly on the modular sofa, hands buried in the pockets of his robe, staring down at the binders and her open notebook still lying all over the flokati rug where she'd left them. He was so deep in thought that he never noticed Arden watching him from the top of the spiral staircase. Something in his manner, remote, deeply private, kept her fom intruding on him. As she got back under the covers, she wondered what he could have been thinking of so intently, and it kept her from going back to sleep. Flint came back to bed in a little while, moving softly so as not to wake her. Pretending to be half-asleep, Arden snuggled up to him. He put his arms around her silently, holding her close, but it was some time before she felt his breathing grow even and deep, before she was caught up in the hypnotic rhythm of it and drifted off to sleep again. The next time she woke up Flint had already left for the mainland without . . .

The piercing ring of the phone shattered Arden's reverie. With a sigh of relief, she rushed over to it, picking up the receiver before the second ring.

"Hi," he said.

"Oh . . . hello," she replied.

Then they both ran out of words at the same time though the feeling between them was palpable.

"I missed you . . . this morning." Arden recovered first. "You must be a very quiet dresser."

Flint cleared his throat in response.

"Although I'm sure even a hurricane couldn't have woken me up this morning," she teased warmly, "I was sleeping so deeply."

"I can't imagine why," he muttered wryly.

A soft, warm flush spread over Arden as she remembered exactly why, and she couldn't wait to see him again. "Where are you?" she asked lightly, scanning the cove through the window for the seaplane, but there was still no sign of it.

"We're on our way back. We should be there in less than an hour," he informed her in an impersonal tone of voice which puzzled her until she remembered that there were other people present and he wasn't free to talk. "I'm calling to make sure you'll be at the dinner party tonight. We've got some very interesting guests and I'd like you to be there."

"All right," Arden agreed halfheartedly. She was hoping they'd have dinner alone at the lighthouse. The last thing she wanted was to have other people around.

"You'll be there then," he insisted. "Cocktails at seven by the pool. I have a little . . . surprise for you."

"A surprise?" Arden laughed, astonished. "What kind of surprise?"

"It wouldn't be much of a surprise if I told you."

"Please tell me . . . I hate surprises."

"I'm sure you're going to *love* this one."

Arden thought she detected a note of sarcasm in his tone, but before she could question him, he'd hung up. She decided that it was just his way and tried to puzzle out what his surprise could be as she started getting ready for the dinner party.

By the time she'd finished dressing, Arden was sure it could only be one thing: he'd bought her an expensive gift, probably a piece of jewelry. She hoped she was wrong because it hurt her just to think about it. She couldn't believe he'd put her in the same class as Gayle or Felicia, that he'd reduce what they shared last night to the kind of encounter he was used to: favors bought and sold. Despite his bitter experiences with women, his distorted view of them as mercenary creatures, he must know that she'd given herself to him out of the deepest love, deeper than even she would have believed herself capable of before last night. She was sure Flint knew. Hadn't she seen it reflected in his bewildered eyes when she was making love to him?—a kind of fearful wonder.

Arden warned herself about jumping to conclusions as she put the finishing touches on her makeup, but she was sorry now that she'd agreed to go to the dinner party. She was too keyed up emotionally and she knew she didn't fit in with the shallow crowd that surrounded him. And then, of course, there was Gayle.

Flint had made it clear that his relationship with Gayle was a mutually convenient one. Gayle herself had made it pretty obvious that she really didn't love Flint so much as the security and life-style he provided, yet Arden wasn't ready to face her. It wouldn't have bothered her so much if Gayle knew about her and Flint. It was having to pretend that upset her, and not knowing where it would all end. One of the reasons she'd wanted to spend the evening alone with Flint was to talk about what happened . . . and what was going to happen now.

Arden was sure of only one thing—no matter what happened she would never regret last night. Just thinking about it filled her with indescribable joy. And that joy was responsible for the radiance which she saw in her face when she looked in the mirrored doors of the closet before going down to dinner.

She was wearing the sophisticated, black satin evening gown she'd bought on impulse at Bloomingdale's but had never had the courage to wear. She suddenly realized why. She'd never felt woman enough to carry it off. The deep slash of the V neck made it impossible to wear a bra and the bright red petals of the silk rose pinned to the end of it did little to hide her cleavage. The narrow skirt molded her hips and thighs snugly. The overall effect was sensual but elegant, and for the last time, Arden stifled the doubts she had about wearing it. She wanted so much to be beautiful for him. She'd let her long, golden hair tumble softly over her shoulders, instead of sweeping it up into a more sophisticated style to match the gown, because she knew Flint preferred it that way. She wore a bit more eye makeup than usual but had dabbed on gloss instead of lipstick because her lips were still swollen with last night's kisses. For a moment, she wondered whether anyone would notice. She didn't see how they could miss the glow that still lit her eyes and warmed her skin, giving her a slightly feverish look. But all she really cared about, as she made her way downstairs, was seeing Flint again.

The cocktail party was already in full swing at poolside when Arden stood before the glass doors opening out onto the redwood deck. She caught sight of Flint instantly. He was so outstandingly attractive in his white dinner jacket and black tie that she would have spotted him in a crowd of thousands. Even at that distance, Arden felt the sensuous pull of his personality. It set off a quivering sensation in the pit of her stomach and held her, motionless, in the doorway.

Flint must have sensed that he was being watched intently because he turned his head suddenly, looking over the shoulder of the slim, light-haired man he'd been listening to. His eyes widened noticeably when he saw her, sweeping over her black gown with a combination of surprise and hunger.

The excitement at seeing him again, which propelled Arden over the redwood deck towards him, shriveled up inside her when his guest turned and she came face to face with Flint's "surprise."

"I believe you two already know each other," Flint drawled, putting an end to the painfully awkward pause.

Arden was still too stunned to react. In a daze, she watched the pale blue eyes, which had lost none of their ability to appraise, move over her. She heard the familiar, smooth-as-silk voice say, "This certainly doesn't look like the Arden Stuart I remember," as a smile of genuine surprise rather than studied charm greeted her. A manicured hand was extended to her but all she could do was stare at it.

"You remember Neil Foster, don't you, Arden?" Flint prompted.

Anger freed her enough to be able to return the handshake, even smile politely, but it was all done on automatic pilot. "Of course. How are you, Neil?"

"I'm great. But nothing compared to you," he gushed admiringly, and the disdainful smile froze on Flint's face. "Like the ads say, you've come a long way, baby!"

"She sure has," Gayle agreed coolly, having suddenly materialized from behind them, a glittering vision in gold lamé. Only a tiny frown marred her perfect features while she studied Arden critically. "I see you took my advice."

"What advice?" Flint demanded curtly.

"Oh, just something between us girls." She smiled sweetly, offering Flint one of the piña coladas she was holding while taking a sip of the other.

"No, thanks. I'm having scotch tonight."

"But I made it just for you." Gayle pouted prettily. "It's just the way you like it."

"I prefer scotch tonight," he repeated rudely, signaling one of the butlers carrying trays of assorted drinks. There was another awkward pause and Arden tried to think of a way of getting herself out of this situation as gracefully as possible.

"I'd love a piña colada." Neil smiled charmingly, almost fawningly. "Especially one made by our lovely hostess."

Like a wilted flower under spring rain, Gayle blossomed instantly under the shower of Neil's attention. With a flirtatious smile, she started to hand him the drink when she remembered Flint. "You're sure you don't want it?"

"I don't believe in mixing," he muttered caustically, exchanging the empty rock glass he was holding for a full one. "What about you, Miss Stuart, do you believe in mixing?"

"I'm not a very experienced . . . drinker," Arden parried the obvious double entendre while the butler waited for her to make a choice. "Nothing for me, thanks," she said, having just spotted a perfect way out. "I think I'll have some hors d'oeuvres instead." Turning abruptly, she walked over to the buffet. She'd planned on easing her way back inside the villa from there only to find that Flint had followed her.

"Not very experienced?" he continued relentlessly. "That's hard to believe."

"Believe what you like." Arden shrugged, scanning the delicacies spread before her, which included caviar, a painful reminder of the crazy picnic they'd shared last night.

"Just a very gifted amateur then?"

"That's right!" She spun around to face him, no longer able to control the hurt and anger she felt. "The word *amateur* literally means one who loves. It denotes someone who does something . . . not as a profession . . . or for the money . . . but just for the love of it!"

Before Flint could recover from her outburst, Arden had started towards the entrance. "I'll leave *you* to make my excuses to your . . . charming guests," she tossed over her shoulder at him.

"Oh, no, you don't," he muttered under his breath when he'd caught up with her in a few easy strides, just as she was sailing through the entrance. "I went to a lot of trouble to put this little dinner party together and . . ."

"I hope you enjoy it then," she interrupted coldly, "but don't expect me to be a part of it."

"You *are* part of it." He grabbed her arm with his free hand, stopping her. "Whether you like it or not."

"Let go of me," she said calmly, forcing a bright smile for the benefit of the people watching them, which included Gayle and Neil. "If you don't let go of me, I'll make a scene in front of all your very interested guests."

"No, you won't." He smiled broadly as if she'd just made the most amusing remark. "You're too much of a lady."

"Not when I'm not being treated like one."

"Go ahead, the hell I care." He laughed harshly. "I'm in the mood for a good scene!"

Arden was sure he meant it, just as she knew she was incapable of going through with her bluff.

"I told you," he mocked. Tightening his hold on her, he started maneuvering her towards the dining room, making the kind of gesture, with the hand still clenching his drink, that a host showing off his home would make.

"I don't understand any of this," Arden said miserably when they were far enough away from everyone not to be overheard. She was glad now for the chance to be alone with him so they could talk openly. "Why did you do this? Why did you invite Neil here?"

"What's the matter?" He shrugged, pushing the dining room door open forcefully, spilling some of his drink in the process. "Didn't you like my little surprise? I know how much you love digging up the past. Of course, if I'd known the ever-charming Mr. Foster still had such an effect on you . . ."

Arden was so completely thrown by the absurdity of his statement that it was a moment before she could answer. She never got the chance.

"Mrs. McNally," Flint called across the dining room to the housekeeper busy with last-minute touches. Fot the first time Arden became aware that the immense table which usually dominated the center of the room had been replaced by a number of smaller tables set up in the style of a dinner club. He certainly *had* gone to a lot of trouble, she realized, but why?

"'Yes, Mr. Flint?" With a warm smile, Mrs. McNally came bustling over while he continued maneuvering through the rows of tables. "Miss Arden, how lovely you're looking this . . ."

"Mrs. McNally," Flint interrupted impatiently, "you can announce dinner now."

"Now, Mr. Flint? But dinner isn't scheduled for another half an hour yet."

"Would you please announce dinner, Mrs. McNally?"

The feisty housekeeper was about to protest but took one look at his face and thought better of it. "Surely, Mr. Flint." She exchanged a puzzled glance with Arden on her way out.

"Here we are." Flint set his drink down on the center table.

There were only four place settings on it. Arden didn't have to read the name tags in front of each one to know who would be sitting there.

"I'm not staying for dinner," she insisted angrily. "I don't know what game this is you're playing but . . ."

"Musical chairs?" he asked softly, while sliding hers out for her. "Or, in this case, musical beds?"

"It's not my kind of game!" She tried to pull her arm away, which only made him tighten his grip, pulling her closer to him. As angry as she was, the burning pressure of his hand on her skin, the closeness of his strong, taut body affected her deeply. As if disturbed by the same thing, Flint pushed her away from him abruptly, his eyes raking her body in spite of himself.

"That's quite a dress," he snapped, pushing her in front of the chair. "I'd almost bet you knew Prince Charming was coming to dinner."

"What are you talking about?" Arden pleaded, totally confused. "How can you say that? How could you do such a thing . . . after last night?"

"Last night? What was so special about last night? You were out to get firsthand material for your book, and I kept my promise about giving it to you."

Grabbing onto the table to steady herself, Arden sank into the chair with a soundless gasp.

"I must admit," he added while seating himself directly across from her, "I'm curious about how you're going to rate my performance."

It took every bit of control Arden was capable of to say in a steady voice, "On a scale of one to ten I'd say, sexually, you rate an eleven. But, as a human being, you get minus one."

"One out of two ain't bad." He laughed harshly, reaching for his drink as the guests started filing into the dining room on a wave of excited murmurs.

If Arden had been a condemned prisoner on death row, and that meal her last, it couldn't have been more difficult to swallow. She'd never been any good at the games people play, and the charade going on around her was more than she could bear.

Neil, greatly impressed by what he assumed was Arden's new social status, was nauseatingly charming and attentive towards her, even though she was being merely polite to him. That was when he wasn't trying to ingratiate himself with Flint.

Gayle—who never looked lovelier, and knew it—was acting with more than her usual abandon and possessiveness towards Flint, who indulged her like a spoiled but adorable child.

Flint's main concern seemed to be in drawing out Neil, who never realized he was being shown up as vain and shallow—something Arden had never noticed before. She wondered whether Flint was doing it for that reason. Except for an occasional sardonic comment, he deliberately ignored her, yet Arden had the feeling that he was aware of every emotion churning behind the cool facade she managed to maintain.

When dinner was mercifully over, and everyone had retired to the main salon for after-dinner drinks, Arden seized the first socially acceptable moment to make her excuses and leave. Since Flint was standing near the doorway directly in front of the staircase leading up to the guest rooms, Arden was forced to go out the back way.

Feeling like the governor's reprieve had finally come through, she stepped onto the redwood deck and took the first free breath in hours.

"Can I come out to play?" a suave voice inquired from behind her.

Cursing under her breath, Arden turned without bothering to hide the look of annoyance on her face. "I came out here to be by myself, Neil."

"I thought it was to give us a chance to finally be alone." He smiled charmingly, sliding the glass door closed.

"Well, you thought wrong." Over his shoulder

Arden noticed Flint watching them from across the salon. "Please leave me alone." As much to get away from him as from Flint's piercing gaze, she turned and walked briskly down the deck, her heels clicking angrily on the wooden slats as she rounded the corner and went across to the front of the villa. Stepping off the deck onto the pebble driveway, she continued over to the rustic gazebo, perched like an eagle's nest on the edge of the cliff overlooking the southern tip of the cove.

The rough-hewn pillars of the gazebo were spaced widely apart, but the tropical vines climbing up to the pagoda-style roof formed a wall of leaves around her, adding to the feeling of total seclusion. Arden settled into one of the wicker armchairs, putting her feet up on another, and closed her eyes. She relaxed and let the vine-fragrant breeze and soft night sounds wash over her. She'd never realized how much she'd come to love this part of Flint's world. Almost as much as she hated the other and . . .

"I hope I'm not intruding," Neil's voice insinuated itself into her thoughts.

With a harsh sigh, Arden dragged her eyes open reluctantly. He was leaning casually against one of the pillars, holding a brandy snifter in each hand. With the amber light from the Japanese lanterns playing on his elegant features, he looked like an advertisement for an expensive cognac.

"I've been waiting all evening for the chance to talk to you alone," he explained with easy charm.

"We have nothing to say to each other, Neil."

"I think we do. Besides, there's no point in wasting

157

good brandy," he added as he walked over to her. "I brought this out just for you . . . as a kind of peace offering."

"Thanks, but I don't want it. Will you just go away?"

"I would but . . ." Pausing dramatically, he put the snifter down on the wicker table in front of her, gazing at her with a truly tragic expression. "But I'd hate to make the same mistake twice. I did that once, remember? And I've lived to regret it . . . bitterly."

"Well, you know what they say," Arden said drily. "Be careful what you wish for, you might get it."

He seemed surprised by her response and must have decided that a change in tactics was needed because he brightened considerably. "I really can't get over the way you've changed. Whenever I think of you—which is a lot—I remember that sweet young thing who'd just come to the big city. You were so shy and naïve . . ."

"I was naïve all right." Arden couldn't help laughing at herself the way she was then.

"I really can't believe that you, of all people, would end up doing so well for yourself," he blurted out.

"Oh? Am I doing so well for myself?" Arden asked evenly.

"What I meant is," he said, flashing his most charming smile at her, "you've gone and turned into this gorgeous, sophisticated young woman who . . ."

"*You* haven't changed at all," Arden interrupted, because it suddenly occurred to her that he was doing the same old routine, though it was getting a bit worn around the edges. Or maybe it just didn't work with her anymore. And, although he was now in his late thirties, he looked almost a decade younger. It wasn't just the all-American-boy features. His face was remarkably smooth, unlined, as if it hadn't been used much. The pale blue eyes held no depths, just as there was no real warmth or joy in the Pepsodent-perfect smile.

"I must have been out of my head to let you go," he was murmuring intensely, "because . . ."

"What do you want, Neil?"

"Excuse me?"

"You want something from me. What is it?"

"What makes you say that?" He laughed but it had a hollow sound to it.

"Because what *I* remember about you is that you were always at your most charming when you wanted something."

"But what could I possibly . . ."

"You want me to use what you think is my influence with Flint Masters to help you land his account. That's it, isn't it?"

"No . . . of course not," he protested, looking truly offended, "not really. I'm not going to say that I wouldn't be darn grateful for any help you'd care to give me. Landing his account for our company would be quite a coup for me . . ." He paused as if aware of the genuine excitement in his voice. Sitting on the edge of the chair her feet were resting on, he leaned towards her earnestly. "But what I'm really excited about is that with an account this size I'd have to spend a great deal of time down here in the keys."

He leaned closer still, smiling seductively. "We could get to see quite a lot of each other again."

"Oh? And how would your wife feel about that?"

"I told you," he explained, sighing dramatically, "that marriage was a mistake right from the start . . . a total disaster. I'd get a divorce if it wasn't for her father and the children. As it is, we've opted for an open marriage."

"An open marriage . . . Jessica? She's one of the most possessive women I've ever met."

"Tell me about it," he groaned. "But, luckily, most of our friends are into it and you know Jessie. She's always up on the 'in' thing. I've got to give her that much."

"Sounds terrific." Arden laughed sarcastically.

The sarcasm went right over his head; he obviously interpreted the laugh as her acceptance because he jumped up excitedly. "Then you'll do it?" he exclaimed enthusiastically. "I can't tell you how great this makes me feel! It's like getting a second chance in life. Landing this account and seeing you again . . ." He was so overwhelmed that he couldn't go on.

"I'm very glad I got to see you too, Neil," Arden replied sincerely, "because I never realized till now what a phony, manipulative, calculating son of a bitch you really are."

"What?" The smile wavered on his lips for a second, threatening to collapse, but at the last moment turned into an even bigger, more charming smile. Except for the right corner, which twitched, refusing or unable to go up. "Come on, Arden, you're not still mad at me about Jessie?"

"Oh, go away, Neil," she muttered disgustedly. "Go back to New York. Flint Masters will never give you his account . . . even if he had been considering it. Unlike me, he only needed a couple of hours to size you up. And if you were half as clever as you think you are, you'd have realized it at dinner tonight."

With an exhausted sigh, Arden leaned her head back on the chair as everything that happened today finally got to her. Her eyes closed all by themselves so she didn't see Neil leave. Nor could she have known that he went back inside the villa through the front entrance, going directly up to his room so everyone who'd seen them leave the party together wouldn't realize he'd struck out with her. She wasn't conscious of the passage of time either as she took advantage of the solitude to sort out the confusing events of the last few days.

Arden still couldn't reconcile the passion and tenderness of Flint's lovemaking last night with the deliberately contemptuous way he treated her earlier. Nor could she understand why he invited Neil here. In a strange way, she was glad now that he had. Finally seeing the kind of man Neil was had severed the last tie that had been binding her to that painful memory from her past. All this time, she'd blamed herself for Neil's jilting her. She'd been convinced that it was because of her lack of sophistication and sexual experience. And she'd felt less of a woman because of it. Until last night.

Last night with Flint she'd felt as desirable, as loving, as complete as a woman could feel. And for that, she'd always be grateful to him. But she

161

couldn't live with the contempt he obviously had for her. Did he really believe she went to bed with him just to get information for the book?

Arden couldn't help thinking how ironic it was that the book, which had first brought them together, was now responsible for destroying whatever happiness they might have had—especially since she was finally able to admit to herself that she hadn't really come here because of the book, but because of the man who had fascinated her for almost two years before she had ever met him. And who would go on fascinating her, she knew now, even though she'd never see him again after tonight.

11

The party had moved outside to the pool again and Flint was nowhere in sight when Arden returned to the villa, so she had no trouble slipping upstairs, unnoticed. Closing the door to her room behind her, she let out a sigh of relief, only to draw it in again sharply when she saw Flint pacing the floor like a caged tiger.

He came to a halt when he saw her and, trying to effect a casual pose, raised his glass in a mocking toast. "Ah, Cinderella back from the ball," he drawled sarcastically. "Did you have a ball with Prince Charming?"

"What are you . . ."

"You just couldn't wait to jump back into bed with him, could you?" he muttered contemptuously before finishing off his drink in one gulp.

Too emotionally drained by the events of the day even to attempt a response, Arden just shook her head in disbelief.

"What? No protestations of innocence?" he mocked, covering the distance between them in a few unsteady strides.

"No."

He went pale under his tan. "You . . . admit it then?"

"No," Arden murmured sadly, "I'm just through trying to defend myself to you, Flint. It seems that's all I've done . . . since we first met. First over the book with Felicia . . . then this book. You've even accused me of making love with you just to get some information about your past, and now . . . this." She paused to search his troubled face intently. "You seem determined to think the worst of me. Why?"

"Very clever: a good offense is the best defense," he allowed caustically, "but it's not going to work. I want to know where the hell you were for nearly two hours. I looked for you everywhere . . . everywhere! Like an idiot . . . a crazed fool!" He turned away from her, trying to hide the anguish on his face and get himself back under control.

"Flint, I . . ."

"I know where the ever-charming Mr. Foster was," he cut her off coldly, "because I saw the lights go on in his room. And that's where you were, wasn't it?"

"Would you believe me if I told you?"

"Try me."

"My God, Flint, if you didn't realize last night the way I feel about you, nothing I can say now could possibly convince you!"

"I know where you were, dammit! I just want to hear you say it!"

Pulling herself up proudly, Arden walked back over to the door and opened it. "You shouldn't judge other people by yourself," she said with ice-cold fury. "Just because you can jump from one bed to another doesn't mean I can."

"Is that why you did it . . . because you thought I was still sleeping with Gayle?" he asked incredulously, as if he'd never considered the possibility. "But I haven't been with her since I came back from Miami with you . . . not once."

"That's not how it looked at dinner tonight. I've never seen her more . . . amorous. She couldn't keep her hands off you!"

"That was all an act." He shrugged contemptuously. "She's just afraid of losing a meal ticket . . . and don't change the subject!"

"But it *is* the subject," Arden murmured intensely, feeling as though she'd just stumbled onto the last missing pieces of the puzzle. She closed the door again, without even realizing it, while she struggled to fit the pieces together. "This contempt you have for all women is exactly the subject. It's the reason you're . . ."

"My contempt is just for one woman," he interrupted bitterly, while pouring himself a double scotch from the bottle he'd brought with him. "I always knew that sweet innocent act of yours couldn't be for real. But you almost had me fooled last night." He took a long, hard swallow. "That was some performance. You should have been an actress instead of a writer."

"That's what you'd like to believe, isn't it?" Arden said slowly, tentatively, as she walked back over to him. The pieces were starting to fall into place, one by one. "You want to believe that I'm just like Gayle or Felicia . . . the kind of woman you always get involved with. Women who can't love, who only care about money and status . . . who prefer sex without emotion. That way you're safe . . . you don't have to love back. Because really loving somebody scares the hell out of you."

"I didn't come here to listen to any more of your Freudian pop psychology," he muttered angrily, but it was clear that her words had a deeply unsettling effect on him. "You still haven't given me a straight answer about you and Mr. Charming."

"And *that's* why you invited Neil here," Arden suddenly realized. "It was a kind of . . . love test. You wanted to make sure of my feelings for you before you let yourself love me, because you're afraid I'll run out on you like your mother and your fiancée."

"Well, you sure flunked *that* test, didn't you?" He laughed harshly, slamming the glass down on the table as he started to brush past her.

"No, I didn't . . . and you know it!" Arden cried, stepping directly in front of him so he was forced to deal with her. "Flint, you know you don't really believe I made love with Neil," she pleaded softly, "or that I even care about him anymore. You can't believe that . . . not after last night."

The anguish in the depths of his charcoal-dark eyes told her how much he wanted to believe her, yet some part of him was still fighting it. "Then why were you so shaken when you first saw him if he no longer means anything to you?" he agonized. "You were so upset all through dinner that you could barely swallow your food!"

"Oh, my God, it was because of *you* I was so upset," she cried desperately. "You didn't call me all day and then when you did, you were so impersonal . . . as if last night had meant nothing to you. And it wasn't seeing Neil again that bothered me, it was the fact that you brought him here and practically threw him at me and then all through dinner you treated me with such contempt and . . . and Gayle was hanging all over you and . . ." Arden burst into tears as the emotions she'd been suppressing all day finally overwhelmed her.

"Don't . . . don't do that," he pleaded as if she were hurting him somehow. "Come on . . . don't." He started wiping the tears away with sandpaper thumbs, with hands that covered her whole face. Arden gasped at their burning tenderness and stopped crying as suddenly as a child scared out of the hiccups. A tear slid down her face and, slipping past his fingers, got caught in the corner of her mouth. He moved to wipe it away but licked it up with his tongue instead before his mouth crushed hers with a fierce tenderness.

A broken-off sob caught in her throat, turning into a low moan as soothing fingers moved from her face to lose themselves in the golden mass of her hair and hold her softly captive. She shivered as she felt the barely suppressed hunger beneath his gentleness in the achingly tender kisses with which he was covering her tearstained face. When his lips found hers again, the salty taste of her tears mingled with the mellow flavor of scotch and the moist, sweet taste of him.

Even if she'd wanted to, she'd have been unable to resist the intensity of feeling he projected and evoked in her. As always, it was a passion that dissolved reason. Wrapping herself around him, her lips parted under his as everything in her opened up to him.

"Oh, lover," he groaned on her mouth, more from gratitude than desire. Gathering her up impulsively in his strong arms, only to cling to her as if for support, Flint hid the naked emotion on his face in the hollow of her shoulder, in the tangled silk of her hair. But he couldn't hide the quivering in every muscle of his taut body. It vibrated all through her, setting off a ripple effect deep inside which spread to her farthest nerve endings, releasing a surge of love that left her shaking uncontrollably in his arms.

"This is what . . . drove me out of my mind when I . . . couldn't find you," he muttered brokenly, trailing desperate little kisses the length of her slender neck, "the thought of you . . . with him . . . like this."

"But it was never like this . . . never!" Arden cried breathlessly. "Only with you. It's all *you* . . . don't you know that yet?" Flint's head jerked back to look up at her with disbelieving, tormented eyes. "I've never been . . . like this. I never knew I could be till I met you." A lifetime of doubt was still fighting the longing to believe in his eyes and Arden hurt for him—for both of them. "Flint, please believe me, I love you," she begged through a fresh mist of tears. "I love you so much, I . . . I hurt."

With a sharp intake of breath, a strangled cry, Flint sank to his knees before her. His face looked as though it were all in pieces. He buried it between her breasts, crushing her to him so hard that Arden could barely breathe. Yet she tangled both hands in his hair to hold him even closer. She held him for a timeless moment, his face burning through the thin satin fabric of her gown.

When he finally looked up at her again, his face was composed but unnaturally flushed, his eyes dark with longing. His sensuous lips moved, forming soundless words. Arden ached to hear them, was sure he was on the verge of saying them at last. Instead, his lips began tracing the deep slash of her V neckline with avid kisses.

Arden gasped as his hands moved from her back to her breasts. Still sensitive from last night, they responded instantly to his touch, to the message his tongue repeated insistently right through the delicate fabric of her gown. The satin seemed to fuse with her breasts under the heat of his mouth until it felt like a second skin, her still-tender nipples straining to bursting under it. Two warm, wet circles outlined their aching tautness when his mouth continued hungrily down the front of her body.

Blindly, his fingertips reached up, skimming along the edge of her neckline up to her shoulders where they hooked into the narrow straps to begin peeling the gown slowly but urgently down her trembling body. His ravenous mouth and hands never stopped moving over her as he finished undressing her. He seemed to be as helplessly driven by the force of his need for her as she was overwhelmed by it.

She experienced the most exquisite pleasure she'd ever known and nothing else existed beyond it. All of reality had narrowed down to a single atom of flesh quickening under the relentless, tantalizing assault of his tongue as it searched out and found the most sensitive, secret part of her. Arden felt herself dissolving utterly. Her own moans came back to her as an echo while he inscribed a searing, indelible message of love and desire over every inch of her.

Stopping only to tear off his own clothes, Flint carried Arden over to the brass bed, not even bothering to turn down the covers in his eagerness to complete their union. He made love to her with a desperate urgency, as if he meant to imprint himself on her forever, to wipe out the memory of any other man and destroy the possibility of her ever wanting another.

Afterwards, he held her in his arms, silently. Once again, Arden felt instinctively that there was something he wanted to tell her. She sensed him struggling to find the words yet unable to say them. It hung there between them, as palpable as the perspiration gleaming on their skins still gluing their bodies together wherever they touched.

Running her fingers through the damp curls on his chest, she tipped her head back over the strong shoulder it was resting on to study his thoughtful face. "What are you thinking about so seriously?"

"The words of a poem, would you believe?" He chuckled softly at himself.

"A poem?"

"Yeah . . . but I can only remember one line: 'Come live with me and be my love . . .'"

"'And we will all the pleasures prove . . .'"

"Umm, we sure will." He squeezed her playfully as he nibbled on her earlobe. "So will you?"

"Stop . . . that tickles." She giggled, squirming around in his arms. "Will I what?"

"Come live with me and be my love?"

"Are you . . . serious?" she asked breathlessly, her sapphire eyes widening in amazement.

"Sure. There's nothing for you back in New York, is there? You can write just as easily here as there . . . more easily, because here I can provide anything you want or need. And with all my contacts, I know I could help your career so . . ." He paused as he felt her stiffen in his arms. "Something wrong?"

"Don't do this to me, Flint," she pleaded softly, "not now."

"Do what? What do you mean?"

"You're treating me like one of your . . . kept women again."

"Why? Because I want to take care of you . . . and give you anything you want?"

"*You're* all I want . . . *you*. Can't you get that through your head?"

"Well, I'm part of the deal." He laughed.

"Deal? Is that what it would be like with us? Is that what you're offering me . . . a deal?"

"That's just a figure of speech, Arden; don't make such a big deal out of . . . damn!" With a disgusted sigh, he dragged the long, muscular leg that was wrapped around hers away. It dropped onto the mattress with a dull thud. "Look, maybe I didn't get the words right . . . but you know how I feel about you."

"No . . . I don't," she murmured ruefully. "Tell me."

"I've never . . . felt about anyone . . . ever . . . the way I feel about you."

"But what do you feel? Love . . . hate . . . lust . . . what?" She searched his narrowing eyes for the answer he seemed unable to give her as the love-softened lines of his face started to harden. "You can't even say the word, can you?"

"You're the expert with words . . . not me," he muttered uncomfortably, his warm hand releasing the breast he'd been holding so tenderly. He ran it through his hair, which she'd done a pretty thorough job of mussing. "Look, this is all very new to me. I'm sorry if I'm not doing a good job of it."

"What's new, Flint?" Arden smiled sadly. "You're just trying to replace Gayle with me, just like you replaced Felicia with Gayle and the girl before that with Felicia."

"That's not true," he protested. "It's not the same."

"It's the same . . . arrangement, don't you see that? It's the perfect way to have me while still keeping me at a safe distance. You're offering me everything but yourself . . . because you're still afraid to love."

"Then I wouldn't be asking you to live with me, but *this* is how I live," he insisted, pulling his arm from around her shoulders. "It's how I've always lived. I wouldn't know any other way." Sliding out of her embrace completely, he sat up against the brass headboard, studying her with a mixture of annoyance and confusion. "Don't you want to come and live with me?"

"Yes, very much! But I want to live with *you*, not with you and a . . . a cast of thousands!"

"I don't know what you want from me," he muttered, getting to his feet in one impatient motion, leaving her stranded in the middle of the huge bed. "Do you expect me to change my whole life for you?"

"No, of course not . . . and I don't want anything *from* you either. All I want is for us to have a loving and honest relationship—a relationship, not an arrangement!"

With a deepening frown, Flint walked over to where their clothes were lying in a heap on the carpet.

"But how can you have a relationship with someone," Arden continued intensely, "if you're surrounded by a houseful of strangers day and night and involved in an endless round of parties?"

Instead of answering her, he began separating their clothes into his and hers piles.

"But that's the whole point to your kind of lifestyle," she added sadly, "isn't it?"

He shot her the strangest look before answering defensively, "Why don't you just say that you don't care enough about me to want to live with me?"

"Because it's not true, Flint. I love you . . . more than I ever knew I could love anyone. But I'd rather end it now than watch that love being destroyed bit by bit . . . which is what would happen. And I . . . I just couldn't take that."

He turned his attention back to the clothes again, so Arden couldn't tell what effect her words had had on him. Her damp skin, which had been warmed by his body when they were snuggling up, had turned cold and clammy. She pulled up the sheet lying at the foot of the bed where he'd tossed it impetuously and covered herself up, hugging herself to keep warm while she watched him. He dressed quickly, silently, moving in that powerful yet graceful way of his. He was so beautiful to her that it hurt to look at him.

When Flint was through dressing, he made for the door without so much as a glance in her direction, then hesitated as he was about to step through the doorway. Once again, Arden sensed that he longed to say something to her. She could see it in the tense muscles in his back, the whitening knuckles of his hand as it clenched the doorknob.

"Looks like we've both got a lot of heavy thinking to do," he mumbled over his shoulder just before he closed the door behind him.

12

·<del>·<del>··<del>··<del>··<del>·

Arden realized that it wasn't a particularly good beach day as she spread her towel out on the pearl-colored sand. The sun was warm and brilliant but it kept cutting in and out of the huge clouds that were rapidly taking over the sky, and the strong breeze had an unusual chill to it. She decided to stay anyway. Up at the villa, the partying had already begun, earlier than usual even for a Saturday. At least here she'd be able to relax and think clearly . . . or, better still, not think at all. Her head ached from thinking too much, since that's how she'd spent most of last night. The few times she'd drifted into a fitful sleep, she merely continued in her dreams arguing the pros and cons of living with Flint.

Unexpected memories flooded her at the sight of the raft bobbing up and down in the choppy water as she peeled down to her bathing suit. Arden suddenly realized that this was the last place she'd be able to stop thinking about Flint and that her real reason for coming down to the deserted beach was to chance seeing him again.

He hadn't shown up at breakfast or lunch, and his yacht was still anchored in the marina, even though he never failed to go sailing on weekends. She assumed that he'd decided not to sail because of the dark storm clouds hovering on the horizon and the distant thunder rumbling in over the waves from the direction of Key West.

As she settled onto the beach towel, Arden wondered whether Flint was in the lighthouse. Glancing up at it, she was surprised to see what looked like the outline of a man standing out on the metal observation deck. By the time she sat up again and shaded her eyes against the sun's glare with her hand he was gone . . . if he'd ever been there.

With a waery sigh, Arden dropped the glasses back into her beach bag, which she then used as a pillow to rest her head on. Just as the wind whipped the sea into high foamy crests, the sight of the lighthouse was churning up deeply disturbed feelings inside her. Though, admittedly, she'd spent the happiest moments of her life within those circular walls, she couldn't help resenting it tremendously. That lighthouse, she realized, was like an ivory tower

Flint had created in which to hide from the rest of the world. It served to shut out the pain and disappointment he feared, but it also locked out whatever chance of love and happiness he might have. She was amazed that he had let her in there.

But he had. He had reached out to her through his pain and fear, even if it was in the only way he knew, a way which precluded his making a total commitment. Maybe once he realized how much she loved him . . . so much that she was willing to accept him on his terms, to cherish whatever he was able to give her of himself in spite of her own doubts and fears. . . .

Arden sat up abruptly. She was like Flint, she realized suddenly. She'd been living in an ivory tower also. Hers wasn't a real one, like Flint's it was inside her. And she carried it with her everywhere she went. She'd started building it, stone by invisible stone, when she lost her family. And when her one attempt to venture out of it, with Neil, had ended in rejection, she locked the door and threw away the key.

Flint had been right about her, after all. She'd buried herself in her writing, choosing to observe life rather than live it. It was ironic that *he* should be the one to breach the walls of her ivory tower, to make her experience a depth of love and desire she had never known she was capable of. Leaving him now would be like walling herself up alive again, which was another reason why . . .

The sensation of raindrops on her skin interrupted Arden's thoughts. She'd been so involved that she hadn't noticed that the line of storm clouds hovering on the horizon had taken over the sky completely. The large, individual drops were warm as they splattered on her body but quickly turned cold in the chilling wind. A flash of lightning zigzagged across the sky, followed by a deafening thunderclap. As if the lightning had split the sky wide open, the uneven, separate drops suddenly became part of a solid wall of rain.

Jumping up from the beach towel, which was already as soaked as she was, Arden started quickly gathering her things together. There was no shelter on the beach and it was a long climb up to the villa. She was trying to decide what to do when she heard her name carried on the wind. Following the sound, she looked up to see Flint calling and waving her over to him as he hurried down the jetty under a beach umbrella.

Clutching her drenched things to her as best she could, Arden ran to him, fighting the wind and rain all the way. Wrapping his free arm around her shoulders, Flint gathered her under the enormous umbrella and together they made a run for the lighthouse as another bolt of lightning split the sky.

Slamming the door on the rumble of thunder that followed, Flint dropped the soaked-through umbrella on the stone floor of the foyer. "Just drop everything . . . right here."

"I don't . . . believe that." Arden laughed in short gasps, letting everything tumble out of her arms. "It happened . . . so fast."

"Storms come and go pretty quickly here in the keys." His silvery gaze skimmed over her half-nude body. "Come on, let me get you something to put on . . . you're all gooseflesh."

"But I'm soaking wet and covered with sand. I'll track everything up."

"Don't worry about it." Taking her arm, he propelled her up the spiral staircase without another word or look. When they reached the top floor, he guided her gently but firmly into the colorful, Spanish-tiled bathroom.

"You'll find fresh towels on the rack there. Shampoo and blow-dryer in that cabinet. Call me if you need anything." He sounded as formal as a hotel clerk. Arden wondered if he was still angry with her about last night. "I'll go put some more logs on the fire and get you something to wear," he added politely, before closing the door behind him.

It didn't take long for Arden to wash the sand off herself, but she lingered in the shower trying to find the words to tell Flint that she'd changed her mind about living with him. She was still rewriting them in her head, as she finished blow-drying her hair into a halo of golden curls, when he reappeared.

He'd changed into a pair of dry jeans that fit him like a second skin, but still wore the velour top that matched his pale gray eyes and softly molded every muscle underneath. The palms of her hands tingled with the memory of those sleek, warm muscles and her mouth went dry. Once again, Arden was amazed at how aware she was of him physically, how deeply she was affected by the sensual and emotional intensity he projected so effortlessly.

"I'm afraid this is the best I can do." He offered

her his maroon silk bathrobe. "But I think I like that outfit better," he added wryly, indicating the bath towel she'd wrapped around her like a sarong. With a murmured thanks, Arden slipped into the robe and, holding it closed with one hand, tugged the towel out from under it with the other. His amused smile told her how foolish her modesty was and reminded her that he'd already explored every inch of her.

A sudden burst of laughter from him lightened the heavily charged atmosphere as Arden finished tying the robe. "What's so funny?"

"You . . . in that robe."

Looking at herself in the full-length mirror, she had to admit that he was right. The sleeves of the bathrobe hung four or five inches below her finger-tips and the hem, which would have come to his ankles, formed a silken pool around her feet.

"Here . . . let me," he said, reverting to his polite but distant tone of voice as he proceeded to roll the sleeves up. He had to bend down to do it and Arden caught the scent of balsam from his hair.

"Thanks." She lifted the front of the robe up with both hands but the back got tangled around her ankles when she attempted to walk.

"Better let me," Flint insisted. "We don't want you tripping down the stairs." Before she realized what he was doing, he'd swung her high into his arms and was carrying her out the door. After an initial moment of surprise, Arden wound her arms around his neck, letting her body relax into his as he began the descent to the living room. Closing her eyes, she clung to him tightly as the walls went spiraling around her, losing herself in the strong, safe feel of his arms, the warm, tangy scent of him. Being in his arms was like coming home. Arden knew she'd made the right choice. How could something that felt so right be wrong?

Peeking up at Flint through her lashes, Arden was about to tell him that she'd changed her mind about living with him, that she knew now that she couldn't live without him. But something about the set of his rugged jaw, the closed look in his eyes as they concentrated on the winding steps kept her from going on. He might have been carrying a sack of potatoes, she realized ruefully, he seemed so unaware of her. Yet when he set her back on her feet in front of the modular sofa, she thought she felt his hands trembling as they slid down her back to circle her waist. She couldn't be sure because the strong, warm feel of them through the thin fabric of the robe had sent a shiver up her spine.

"Flint, I . . ."

"Get over to the fire," he ordered, releasing her with a tiny push in that direction. "I'll get you a cognac. That'll warm you up. I know you don't think much of our life here," he tossed off sarcastically on his way over to the bar, "so I'd hate for you to catch cold because of it."

The impulse she'd had to tell Flint how much she loved him shriveled up inside her as Arden sank down onto the flokati rug. The sound of the rain and wind rattling the windows, the waves crashing against the rocks, was magnified by the tense silence between them, a silence Arden felt incapable of breaking for fear of another sarcastic put-down.

He was standing just across the room from her, yet she had the impression that they were separated by a vast, insuperable distance. They were both withdrawing into their separate towers again, she realized suddenly. She could see the wall going up around him as he stiffly poured the cognac, could almost hear the sound of the door slamming shut, the metal click of the bolt.

Arden wound her fingers unconsciously in the long, fleecy strands of the carpet. Flint had reached out to her last night, even if it was in the only way he knew, she reminded herself, and she'd turned him down. Knowing how proud he was, he wouldn't reach out to her again. For once in her life, *she* was going to have to do the reaching.

"Flint, I . . . I've thought over what we talked about last night . . . about living together?"

His hand hesitated for a fraction of a second before he finished pouring a second cognac. "So did I. What did *you* come up with?" he said tightly as he carried the drinks over to her. "Not any more facts, I hope."

"Just one." Arden accepted the snifter but chose to ignore the sarcasm this time. She knew now that it was just his way of trying to protect himself. "The fact is that I love you very much. And I couldn't leave you now even if I tried."

"Does that mean that . . . you're willing to come and live with me?" he asked incredulously as if it were the last thing he'd expected from her.

"Yes."

His perplexed frown deepened as he stepped over to the fireplace. Standing with his back to her, he stared silently into the smoldering fire for some moments.

"You still want me to come live with you," Arden asked breathlessly, "don't you?"

"I thought you said you wouldn't be happy living my way," he answered, reaching casually for the poker.

"I know I'd be happy when I'm with you. I'll just have to work out the rest of it somehow."

He started poking at the logs, as if he were jabbing away at some obstacle, sending sparks flying in all directions. "You'd be willing to do that . . . for me?" He gave her a long, intense look over his shoulder.

"Yes, for you . . . but for me, too." Arden smiled lovingly. "I can't imagine my life without you anymore, Flint. And I don't want to go back to the way it was before I met you."

His silvery eyes misted over, but Arden was sure the moistness was either from the smoke or an illusion created by the tears of love filling her own eyes. "I did some pretty heavy thinking too," he said finally, sliding the poker back into its antique brass holder. "And you were right." Stepping back to where Arden was sitting on the carpet, he hunkered down next to her, cupping his brandy glass in both hands. "Living together wouldn't work . . . not for us. We'd have to either . . . get married . . ."

"What?"

". . . or break it off completely, like you said. You were right about . . . just about everything." He laughed harshly before taking a long, hard swallow of cognac. "You do scare the hell out of me, lady."

"But why? Because I love you so much?"

"No." He smiled wryly into the amber liquid he was swirling around in the glass. "Because I love you so much."

"You . . . do?" Arden gasped ecstatically. "You . . . love me?"

"I never *knew* anybody could love somebody so much," he muttered miserably.

Arden didn't know whether to laugh or to cry. "Is that so awful?"

"Yes! Yes, it's awful!" The sheer force of emotion brought him to his feet. "I don't know where the hell I am or what I'm doing half the time! Ever since I met you I've been totally out of control!"

"It's the same with me . . . I know."

"Before I fell in love with you I felt . . . invulnerable. Nothing could hurt me. My success or failure in life was defined by my work, but now . . ."

"Yes . . . me too."

"All right, I admit my work didn't make me very happy," he conceded as if she were arguing the point, "but . . ."

"Then I *do* make you happy!"

"Happy? Are you kidding?" Flint sank down onto his knees in front of her. "I never knew such happiness existed. I never felt so . . . so . . ."

"Alive."

"Yes, that's it . . . alive!" His silvery eyes glowed with the love he could no longer deny; his whole face was transfigured by it. Blinded by him, all Arden could do was stare. "I told you once that you wrecked me for anybody else," he continued, unable to stop the flow now that the floodgates were open. "When I said it I meant it physically because that's all I knew or cared about then. But it's much more than that. You bring out feelings in me I never knew were there and . . . I'm still not sure how to handle them and it's . . . scary."

Finishing off his cognac in one gulp, Flint set the snifter down on the carpet next to hers. "But I'll tell you what I just realized is even scarier." Reaching out, his fingers softly traced the outline of Arden's cheek. "Going through life without really being alive." Sliding his hand into the golden mass of her hair, he drew her face up to his. "Going through life without *you* really scares the hell out of me," he groaned just before his mouth came down on hers hungrily. Grabbing onto him with every part of her, Arden returned his kiss with all the love that was in her.

"Yes . . . that's it," he moaned on her mouth, "that's what I've always wanted . . . right from that first time. I just couldn't believe it was true."

"Believe it . . . please believe it," Arden implored with tears of joy in her eyes, "even though it is unbelievable . . . so much love."

"I'm sure going to try. You will marry me? I'll close up the villa . . . or we'll keep it open for occasional entertaining and you'll live here in the lighthouse with me. OK?"

"Here . . . in your ivory tower?" she teased warmly. "That's what this is, you know."

"So you figured that one out too, did you?" He laughed.

The storm must have stopped as suddenly as it began because sunlight was streaming through the stained-glass windows, casting a multicolored pattern all over the white carpet as Arden sank down on it, holding her arms out to him.

"Well, from now on it'll be *our* ivory tower," Flint vowed softly, just before he wrapped his arms around her, becoming part of the rainbow with Arden.

YOU'LL BE SWEPT AWAY WITH SILHOUETTE DESIRE

$1.75 each

1 ☐ James

2 ☐ Monet

3 ☐ Clay

4 ☐ Carey

5 ☐ Baker

6 ☐ Mallory

7 ☐ St. Claire

8 ☐ Dee

9 ☐ Simms

10 ☐ Smith

$1.95 each

11 ☐ James

12 ☐ Palmer

13 ☐ Wallace

14 ☐ Valley

15 ☐ Vernon

16 ☐ Major

17 ☐ Simms

18 ☐ Ross

19 ☐ James

20 ☐ Allison

21 ☐ Baker

22 ☐ Durant

23 ☐ Sunshine

24 ☐ Baxter

25 ☐ James

26 ☐ Palmer

27 ☐ Conrad

28 ☐ Lovan

29 ☐ Michelle

30 ☐ Lind

31 ☐ James

32 ☐ Clay

33 ☐ Powers

34 ☐ Milan

35 ☐ Major

36 ☐ Summers

37 ☐ James

38 ☐ Douglass

39 ☐ Monet

40 ☐ Mallory

41 ☐ St. Claire

42 ☐ Stewart

43 ☐ Simms

44 ☐ West

45 ☐ Clay

46 ☐ Chance

47 ☐ Michelle

48 ☐ Powers

49 ☐ James

50 ☐ Palmer

51 ☐ Lind

52 ☐ Morgan

53 ☐ Joyce

54 ☐ Fulford

55 ☐ James

56 ☐ Douglass

57 ☐ Michelle

58 ☐ Mallory

59 ☐ Powers

60 ☐ Dennis

61 ☐ Simms

62 ☐ Monet

63 ☐ Dee

64 ☐ Milan

65 ☐ Allison

66 ☐ Langtry

67 ☐ James

68 ☐ Browning

69 ☐ Carey

70 ☐ Victor

71 ☐ Joyce

72 ☐ Hart

73 ☐ St. Clair

74 ☐ Douglass

75 ☐ McKenna

76 ☐ Michelle

77 ☐ Lowell

78 ☐ Barber

79 ☐ Simms

80 ☐ Palmer

81 ☐ Kennedy

82 ☐ Clay

YOU'LL BE SWEPT AWAY WITH SILHOUETTE DESIRE

$1.95 each

83 ☐ Chance	95 ☐ Summers	107 ☐ Chance	119 ☐ John
84 ☐ Powers	96 ☐ Milan	108 ☐ Gladstone	120 ☐ Clay
85 ☐ James	97 ☐ James	109 ☐ Simms	121 ☐ Browning
86 ☐ Malek	98 ☐ Joyce	110 ☐ Palmer	122 ☐ Trent
87 ☐ Michelle	99 ☐ Major	111 ☐ Browning	123 ☐ Paige
88 ☐ Trevor	100 ☐ Howard	112 ☐ Nicole	124 ☐ St. George
89 ☐ Ross	101 ☐ Morgan	113 ☐ Cresswell	125 ☐ Caimi
90 ☐ Roszel	102 ☐ Palmer	114 ☐ Ross	126 ☐ Carey
91 ☐ Browning	103 ☐ James	115 ☐ James	
92 ☐ Carey	104 ☐ Chase	116 ☐ Joyce	
93 ☐ Berk	105 ☐ Blair	117 ☐ Powers	
94 ☐ Robbins	106 ☐ Michelle	118 ☐ Milan	

SILHOUETTE DESIRE, Department SD/6
1230 Avenue of the Americas
New York, NY 10020

Please send me the books I have checked above. I am enclosing $_____
(please add 75¢ to cover postage and handling. NYS and NYC residents please
add appropriate sales tax). Send check or money order—no cash or C.O.D.'s
please. Allow six weeks for delivery.

NAME_____

ADDRESS_____

CITY_____ STATE/ZIP_____

Coming Next Month

Fabulous Beast by Stephanie James

Before, Tabitha had only studied the elusive beasts of legend. Then she rescued Dev Colter from danger on a remote island and found that she had awakened a slumbering dragon.

Political Passions by Suzanne Michelle

Newly-elected mayor Wallis Carmichael was furious to discover that sensual Sam Davenport was really a Pulitzer Prize winning-journalist. Politics and journalism don't mix—and now she had to find out if he was just another reporter out for a story.

Madison Avenue Marriage by Cassandra Bishop

Famous mystery writer Lily Lansden needed a "husband" for her winery commercial and Trent Daily fit the bill. But when the game of pretend turned into real love could Lily give up her Madison Avenue marriage?

Between the Covers by Laurien Blair

Everything changed between co-authors Adam and Haley when they began writing their ninth book together—a romance. Were they only playing out a story or were they friends now unleashing desires restrained for too long?

To Touch the Fire by Shirley Larson

Raine had loved Jade since she was sixteen—but he was her sister's husband. Now her sister had left him—would his bitterness and her guilt over the past threaten their awakening passions?

On Love's Own Terms by Cathlyn McCoy

Luke Ford had been out of Bonnie's life for seven years. But now her devastating husband wanted a second chance, and Bonnie's common sense was betrayed by a passion that still burned.

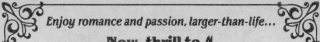